# ASHES TO ASHES

## A CONNOR MAXWELL MYSTERY

TIMOTHY GLASS

CONTENTS

*Other Books by Timothy* vii
*Acknowledgments* xi
*Quote* xiii
*Sundae* xv

| | |
|---|---|
| Chapter 1 | 1 |
| Chapter 2 | 9 |
| Chapter 3 | 18 |
| Chapter 4 | 24 |
| Chapter 5 | 31 |
| Chapter 6 | 37 |
| Chapter 7 | 44 |
| Chapter 8 | 53 |
| Chapter 9 | 60 |
| Chapter 10 | 66 |
| Chapter 11 | 72 |
| Chapter 12 | 80 |
| Chapter 13 | 87 |
| Chapter 14 | 95 |
| Chapter 15 | 103 |
| Chapter 16 | 113 |
| Chapter 17 | 121 |
| Chapter 18 | 130 |
| Chapter 19 | 138 |
| Chapter 20 | 145 |
| Chapter 21 | 153 |
| Chapter 22 | 160 |
| Chapter 23 | 167 |

| | |
|---|---|
| Chapter 24 | 175 |
| Chapter 25 | 182 |
| Chapter 26 | 189 |
| Chapter 27 | 197 |
| Chapter 28 | 206 |
| Chapter 29 | 214 |
| Chapter 30 | 220 |
| Chapter 31 | 228 |
| Chapter 32 | 235 |
| Chapter 33 | 243 |
| Chapter 34 | 250 |
| Chapter 35 | 259 |
| Chapter 36 | 266 |
| Chapter 37 | 272 |
| Chapter 38 | 279 |
| Chapter 39 | 286 |
| Chapter 40 | 292 |
| Chapter 41 | 298 |
| Chapter 42 | 304 |
| Chapter 43 | 312 |
| Chapter 44 | 319 |
| Epilogue | 323 |
| *A Message from Tim* | 329 |
| *About the Author* | 331 |
| *Visit us on the Web* | 333 |

This book is a work of fiction. Any similarity or resemblance to any person, living or deceased, names, places, or incidents is purely coincidental. The work is from the author's imagination.

All rights reserved. No part of the book may be reproduced, stored, or transmitted by any means such as electronic, photocopying, recording, or scanning without written permission from the publisher and copyright owner.

The distribution of this material, by any means over the Internet or copying of this book without prior written permission from the publisher and the copyright owner, is illegal and punishable by law. Platinum Paw Press appreciates your support and respect of the author's rights.

Ashes to Ashes

Written by Timothy Glass

Copyright (C) 2021

Cover art by Timothy Glass

Photograph of Sundae front Cover by Mathew Danver

Library of Congress Control Number 2021909919

ISBN 978-1-7331972-4-3

OTHER BOOKS BY TIMOTHY

**Nonfiction**

Just This Side of Heaven

**Fiction**

Ashes to Ashes, A Connor Maxwell Mystery Book 4

Dancing Queen, A Connor Maxwell Mystery Book 3

Deception, A Connor Maxwell Mystery Book 2

In a Split Second, A Connor Maxwell Mystery Book 1

Dog Knows Best

Postcards

Sleepytown Beagles, Doggone It

Sleepytown Beagles, In The Doghouse

**Children's Fiction**

Sleepytown Beagles, Panda Meets Ms. Daisy Bloom

Sleepytown Beagles, Penny's 4$^{th}$ of July

Sleepytown Beagles, Oh Brother

Sleepytown Beagles, Differences

Sleepytown Beagles, The Lemonade Stand

Sleepytown Beagles, Jingle Beagles

Sleepytown Beagles, Up, Up and Away

*In Memory*

*To Sundae: If ever there was intelligence, beauty, and perfection in a canine companion, you were all that and more. I could have never asked for more. I miss your presence each day as I write. They say a writer's work is filled with many solitary hours but when you were here with me, I was never alone. As I take my early morning walks, I remember how you always led the way. Until we meet again, I miss and love you.*

*In Loving Memory*
*April 27, 2009-December 24, 2020*
*Forever in My Heart*

ACKNOWLEDGMENTS

To Cathy, my wife, for your love and support for what I do every day—and all too often into the night and early mornings. A special thank you to Lisa Dignan Christiansen for your valuable help and information about sign language. To Matt Danver for your help and information about drones. To my wonderful fans and friends for your encouragement and belief in me. A big thanks to the word sleuths who spend hours reading and rereading my material. Lastly, I extend my appreciation to all the four-legged canine officers that serve our country.

QUOTE

When a good man is hurt all would be called good
must suffer with him.
Euripides

SUNDAE

Sundae

CHAPTER 1

The ripple of children's laughter had long since faded as darkness rolled across the city of Lakewood like a blanket covering its young. The days had begun to shorten and the nights lingered longer. September had welcomed a brisk chill early this year and Lakewood homeowners closed their windows to block out the cold. High above the city, the harvest moon shone brightly. It glowed through the bony, naked trees, creating long shadows that formed an eerie pattern on the grassy canvas below.

The home was a large two-by-four structure whose owner had built it some thirty-eight years earlier. Joel Sawyer had constructed the home for his wife, Sylvia, and his young son, Logan. The rambling ranch-style residence was set back from the other houses in a cul-de-sac. The home had a large, well-groomed front yard and a backyard twice the size of any of the others on the street. It was a magnificent yard, laid out with flagstones that curved around the grass and led to an outdoor fireplace, a bricked-in barbeque, and wicker furniture. The backyard bordered a large forest, giving the home even more privacy. Rumor had it that the house at 2255 was the first home to be built on Decker Avenue.

Joel strolled over to his flat-screen TV and began to stream his favorite piano and stringed music. As it played softly in the background, he peered out the living room window and into the darkness. The mirror image of his face shone off the glass. After checking that the front door was locked, Joel eased himself into his favorite chair in front of the fireplace. There, he held a book in his lap and watched the flames dancing before him. His mind took him back in time, to a much happier era when he and his wife, Sylvia, had often sat in this same spot, reading together. She had passed away two years ago. At seventy-eight years of age, Joel knew he would never remarry. He doubted that he would want to remarry even if he were twenty-eight. There would be only one woman in his life and that was his Sylvia. God knew how much he missed her. When his best friend, Fletcher Potts, had lost his wife months later, Joel had invited Fletcher to move in with him and Joel's adopted disabled son, Cole.

---

In the backyard at 2255 Decker Avenue, two deer lazily grazed on the foliage under the moonlight. Suddenly, a window exploded, spewing shards of glass onto the lawn. Flames licked upward around the house's exterior. Both deer looked up, startled at the sound, then bolted in fear back into the forest. Every window in the house glowed as the fire engulfed the interior. The lumber creaked and moaned as the roof gave way and collapsed with a whoosh.

Behind the house, close to the forest, stood a black-clad figure who watched the home burn. Only when the sound of a distant siren became louder did the figure snuff out the cigarette with the toe of his shoe. After taking in one last look at the house fire, he turned and left.

It had been a long day. Detective Connor Maxwell unlocked the door of his unmarked police unit and started the drive home. He had to pick up Sundae, his canine companion, at the vet before they closed. Switching to a country station, Connor brushed a lock of brown hair off his forehead.

As he turned left out of the Lakewood Police Department parking lot, he saw the orange glow of a fire filling the night sky.

"15, PD, has Lakewood Fire Department been dispatched to the westside?"

"Negative, 15," said the Lakewood dispatcher. After hours, the police department dispatchers handled all the police and fire department calls.

"I'm heading over there now. Better get those smoke suckers rolling."

Connor drove toward the glow, turning down two wrong streets before he found his way to Decker Avenue and the burning house. The siren and flashing lights from Connor's car brought the neighbors out from the warm comfort of their homes to watch. Connor quickly gave the address to dispatch and then ran for the garden hose at the side of the house. He peered in the windows, trying to see if anyone was inside, but the fire was too hot and burning out of control. He felt helpless trying to contain a house fire with only a garden hose. One of the neighbors ran to the backyard and used the hose there.

Coughing, Connor ran back to his car, grabbed a rag, and wet it with the garden hose. He wrapped the rag over his nose and mouth while using the garden hose as best he could. By the time the fire department arrived, the house was pretty much a loss. Connor walked across the street, where a cluster of people stood watching the firefighters who tried to contain the relentless blaze.

"Did they make it out?" asked a woman wearing a fluffy pink bathrobe and pink rabbit-eared slippers.

"Can you tell me who lives there?" Connor asked.

"Oh, that would be Joel Sawyer. He's very elderly and…what's his name?" She snapped her fingers as if the movement would cause the forgotten name to flow from her mouth. "Oh, I can't remember his son's name. He has some type of disability. Also, another elderly man lives there, moved in a few years ago after Joel's wife passed…"

Connor left the woman in mid-sentence and ran

back to Kirk Neil, the captain of the fire department. Everyone called him "Captain Kirk."

"There could be three males in the house," Connor yelled to Kirk.

"If there are, they perished in the fire," Captain Kirk said.

Connor pulled the rag back up over his nose and mouth and started for the back door. Captain Kirk grabbed Connor by the shoulders and stopped him.

"Detective, no one would have survived this house fire. All we can do is pray they all went out for the night. Did you ask the people if they saw them in the crowd?"

"Captain, when I got here, no one was standing outside."

Connor returned to the crowd that had gathered on the sidewalk and tried to gather any information he could about the occupants of 2255 Decker Avenue. He took notes from the neighbors as he watched the smoke billow into the sky.

Hours later, when all that remained of 2255 Decker Avenue was a pile of water-drenched rubble,

Captain Kirk and Connor walked through the soggy ash and debris. They found the charred remains of two people.

"Didn't you say Sawyer had an adopted son?" Captain Kirk looked at Connor.

"That's what the lady told me. Said he was disabled, too."

"We have only two bodies here that I can see."

Connor looked down at the two charred sets of remains lying on their sides.

"Guess we'd better have another look-see," Captain Kirk said.

"Do houses usually go up this fast?" Connor asked.

Captain Kirk stopped, studying the debris.

"It almost looks like an accelerant was used. Gas usually burns away, leaving us with very few clues. But the way this fire reacted, I think every room was doused with gas or something."

Captain Kirk began walking through the remains of the house. Still, only two bodies could be accounted for. Connor bent down, examining one of the bodies. He had turned his head to one side to get a better look when he noticed something. Quickly, he pulled a ballpoint pen from his shirt pocket and examined a hole in the back of one of the victim's skulls. Then Connor stood back up and bent down to examine the other victim. Again, the same thing: a hole in the back of the skull.

"Captain, we don't just have a house fire here. We have a double homicide."

CHAPTER 2

The day after the fire at 2255 Decker, the only things left were two burnt-out metal frames of what had once been cars, sitting on a concrete pad in what had been a three-car garage. The fire had gotten so hot that even the tires had burnt away. An expensive die-cast, powder-coated Whitehall mailbox stood to the left of the driveway, proudly displaying the name "Sawyer" in bright white block letters. A mound of charred lumber was all that remained of the lives that had once inhabited this home.

An inquisitive brown squirrel sat high atop the branch of a live oak tree, watching the people digging through the rubble of what had once been a beautiful home. Their actions looked much like those of a bunch of hungry raccoons digging through last night's trash. The Lakewood CSI team sifted through everything they could find, bagging anything that could help solve the mystery of what had happened last night and discarding anything that couldn't. A strip of bright yellow crime scene tape hung from makeshift poles around the debris. In the light morning breeze, it fluttered like a ribbon from a woman's dress.

---

Shortly after midnight, the ME's van had picked up the two sets of remains and transported them to the office of the medical examiner. Both bore toe tags—John Doe 1 and John Doe 2—until a positive identification could be made.

The two sets of skeletal remains lay side by side as the ME, Malcolm Greenblatt, accompanied by Detectives Connor Maxwell and Kate Stroup, removed the white plastic sheet covering the bodies. The blackened skeletons were a stark contrast to the bright stainless-steel tables on which they lay.

"If the lungs were still present, we'd look for

signs of smoke inhalation. As you know, if traces of smoke were present, we'd know that they had been alive before the fire started. A lack of smoke would tell us that they were killed and then the fire was started in an attempt to cover up the murders. However, as you can clearly see, the bodies were subjected to the fire long enough that no organs are left. One thing is clear, though. The bullets entered the back of the skull and exited the front on both sets of remains."

Malcolm Greenblatt pointed to the forehead of the body on the left table. With a white pointer, he indicated what was remaining of the left eye socket. Next to that body was a piece of the skull, to which Malcolm pointed. "I found this last night, next to the body."

Like a puzzle piece, he picked up the shard of skull with his gloved hands and carefully showed both Connor and Kate where the piece belonged. Malcolm then turned to the table at his right and pointed.

"The bullet exited through the nasal cavity area. Due to the smaller bones, I wasn't able to locate any of them. If you want my opinion, and this is only a guess, this victim turned just a little before being shot. Maybe turning to look over his shoulder to see the killer. Whereas," he turned back to the first set of remains, "see, the hole in the forehead is a clean shot."

Malcolm picked up the white pointer again and stuck it through the hole in the back of the skull, then out the gaping hole in the forehead. Next, he turned to the body on the other table and stuck the pointer through the hole.

"This victim, I believe, could have been lying down or knocked down onto the floor when shot. I say this only because of the angle of the shot, which entered the back of the skull and exited through the nose cavity. Also, part of the boney structure beneath the nose along with his front teeth are missing," Malcolm stepped back to allow both detectives to look over the bodies.

"Were you able to get any positive ID on who they are?" Connor asked.

"With the name of Joel Sawyer that you gave me last night, I have one of my assistants checking dental records. We should have something in time. Were you able to get any more information from the neighbors?

"No. We're going back over there today to talk to the neighbors on the street," Connor said as he looked over at Kate. Then he turned back to Malcolm. "Give us a call if you find anything."

Kate Stroup shut the door on their unmarked police unit and looked over at Connor.

"You really know how to treat a girl to breakfast, don't you?" she said as she smiled at Connor.

"Nothing's better than a trip to the ME's office to start your day and work up an appetite." Connor brushed an unruly lock of brown hair from his forehead and looked at his watch. "You hungry?"

"I think I'll pass but you're buying lunch. Can't wait to see where you take me," Kate joked. She looked down at Connor's boots. "New?" She gestured toward them.

"Finally found a pair that fit. Do you know how hard it is to find 3E or 4E width?"

"No, can't say that I do."

---

Connor, Kate, and Sundae parked the car in the driveway, waved at the CSI team, and began canvassing the neighborhood for clues about the occupants of 2255 Decker. The next-door neighbor said that the people had been quiet, with no loud parties. She knew that two elderly men and a young man lived there. Prior to that, the residents had been the elderly man and a woman whom the neighbor believed was the man's wife. The neighbor had heard that the woman had passed away several years ago but other than that, she didn't know much. Kate handed her a card and asked her to call if she thought of anything else.

They knocked at the next door. An elderly man opened it a crack.

"Yes, can I help you?" he asked.

I'm Detective Connor Maxwell and this is my partner, Kate Stroup." Connor showed the man his ID.

"And who is this?" The man opened the door and bent down, looking at Sundae.

"That would be Sundae. She's a Lakewood canine detective," Connor said.

"I'm Louis Nash." The man slowly stood back up, with Kate helping him. "But you can call me Nash. Won't you come in?" He motioned for the trio to enter and gestured to his front living area. "Can I get you anything to drink?"

"No, thank you," both Connor and Kate responded.

"How can I help?" Nash asked as he sat in his

chair. Through his open blinds, he watched the CSI team working across the street.

"Mr. Nash, did you know the people who lived over there?"

"Why, yes. Joel Sawyer, his adopted son, Cole, and Joel's best friend, Fletcher Potts."

Kate quickly noted all the information in her pad.

"Last night, one of the neighbors mentioned that Joel's son was disabled in some way. Were you aware of what type of disability his son had?" Connor asked.

Nash leaned forward, then looked down as if searching for the words to explain.

"Joel and his wife adopted Cole at around seven years of age, I think. The boy was what they call a mute. Couldn't speak a word but smart as a whip. That kid could do math in his head quicker than a calculator! He was a good kid." Nash's eyes teared up.

"Do you know his age now, by any chance?" asked Kate.

"I think he was around seventeen or eighteen."

"And Joel's age? Kate asked.

"We're both the same age, seventy-eight."

"Another neighbor told me last night that Joel had a friend living with him," Connor said.

"As I mentioned earlier, his name was Fletcher. When his wife passed away, Joel asked him to move in with him and Cole. I suspect to help them both cope with the loneliness of losing their wives."

"Getting back to the son, Cole. Do you know why he couldn't talk? Connor asked.

"Cole was in foster care from the time he was a baby. From what I understand, the poor boy had ten different foster parents before Joel and Sylvia adopted him."

Connor cocked his head, thinking as he looked over at the rubble across the street.

"Mr. Nash, did Joel ever mention if there had been any child abuse?" Kate asked.

"Not from Joel and his wife, but when he and the family came over to swim in our backyard pool, I saw burn scars all over the boy's body. I had asked Joel about it later and he said, near as they could tell, the abuse had happened in the last foster home Cole was in. The foster mother was interested only in the state's money, not the well-being of the child. Joel told me that, from what they had learned, in the last foster home Cole was in, someone had crushed Cole's larynx. After that, Cole was made a ward of the state and lived in a home for boys until Joel and Sylvia adopted him."

"Do you know if Joel ever mentioned Cole playing with matches or starting fires as a child or an adult?" Connor asked.

CHAPTER 3

Mr. Nash sat back in his chair, brought his hand to his face in thought, and tapped his index finger against his lower lip.

"Detectives, is this something beyond a house fire? I don't mean to sound like the house fire wasn't tragic enough, but…?"

"Mr. Nash, this is an ongoing investigation. I really can't go into detail other than to say only two bodies were found. You mentioned that three men lived in the house, so we're attempting to piece together the events before the fire and why we found only two bodies," Connor said.

"Both Joel and Fletcher drove. I can clearly see two metal frames of what I assume is left of their cars from my front window. Cole never learned to drive. Either Joel or Fletcher took him to appointments," Nash said, confused by their line of questioning.

"Mr. Nash, I'm sorry for..." Connor was interrupted.

"Can you at least tell me who perished in the fire? You said only two bodies were found," Mr. Nash asked.

"Honestly, no. We're still waiting for positive IDs on the remains we found," Kate interjected.

Mr. Nash clicked his tongue against his teeth, making a "tsk" sound, and shook his head. "From your questions, it sounds like you believe Cole may have had something to do with this." He paused and thought for a second. "Cole came from a troubled background, I'll admit. He was given up as a baby. Shuffled from one foster home to another and abused by the last foster parent. But Joel never said anything to make me believe the boy would harm or kill anyone." Nash leaned back in his chair and looked out the window at what was left of Joel's house.

It had been two days since the fire that had ravished the home at 2255 Decker Avenue. They were still waiting for positive ID on the victims to come back. After Judge Taylor signed off on a warrant to release all of Cole's records to the Lakewood Police Department, Kate began talking to the boys' home where Cole had been placed after living with the last set of abusive foster parents.

As Kate sat at her desk reading the reports about Cole, it seemed to her that Mr. Nash knew only half of Cole's story. She heard the elevator chime and turned to see Connor and Sundae enter. Connor walked to his desk, grabbed a bowl from his bottom drawer, uncapped a fresh bottle of water, and poured it into the bowl for Sundae.

"I'm only partway through Cole's records and it would appear that Sundae has had a better life than Cole," Kate said, turning back to the reports on her desk.

"The reports came in?" Connor asked.

"Oh, did they. I know foster homes are a holding place until someone adopts a child, but for the most part, this poor kid was only a cash cow to most of these people. He was taken back to the state boys' home because he was found in the kitchen eating a slice of bread after the foster parents went to bed.

Or, as they stated, stealing food. When the state received him, he was twenty pounds underweight for his height and age. No charges were ever filed against the foster parents and Cole was put back into the system. The next time the state sent a worker out to check on him, they found marks on his body."

"By marks, do you mean the burns?" Connor asked.

"The report says they looked like belt marks. When the state asked what they were from, the foster parent stated that Cole had talked back to them. This was when he could still speak."

"So, it was correct what Mr. Nash said? That Cole did talk until the damage to his vocal cords?"

"Seems so. Connor, this kid had ten foster homes. Eleven if you count Joel and Sylvia, who were fosters first and then adopted him. He was a ward of the state in the boys' home for a few years after the damage to his vocal cords. No one wanted to foster or adopt him. The records don't come out and state this, but they allude to the fact that Cole was damaged goods."

"Any mention of playing with matches or setting fires?" Connor asked.

"Nothing. The only things Cole likes to do are

read and work on math puzzles. I have a report here from a teacher who states that Cole has college-level math and reading skills. I'm trying to figure out how in the world he has these skills when it seems no one in his life gave a damn about him. The report says that one teacher gave his class a pop quiz. Cole finished it so quickly, the teacher assumed that Cole had cheated. After class, he brought Cole back into the room and gave him another test without any other students present. This was in grade school and Cole finished that test with a hundred percent. The teacher created an algebra quiz. The kid aced it. The teacher said he called Cole up to his desk and gave him an advanced math puzzle book to take home. Cole kept bringing the puzzles back, finished and correct."

Kate looked down at the reports and continued reading. "The teacher purchased adult logic puzzles, even a calculus book. So, while the other kids were doing simple math tests, Cole was given geometry, then calculus problems for his tests." Kate stopped and looked up. "Connor, I took calculus in the twelfth grade and I barely passed! Next, it states that the teacher tried trigonometry. The entries after that are from when Joel and his wife adopted Cole. It seems that because Cole was gifted in math and quite good in other areas, he was able to graduate early. With Cole's gift in math, Joel wanted to further the boy's education. He paid his tuition at New Mexico Tech. Cole didn't want to live at school, so Joel drove him to his classes every day." Kate set down the education section of the report and looked over at Connor.

"Does the report list the foster mom who burned Cole? We could go and have a talk with her and the husband."

Kate flipped through the pages.

"Not by name. This boys' home has only a numbered ID for each foster parent. I can call the home and see if I can get that information. I'm on pretty good terms with the administrator there. She's very worried about Cole."

CHAPTER 4

The Lakewood Police Department received the ME's report early in the morning on the fourth day after the fire. Sandy Curtis, the head of dispatch, delivered the report to Kate's desk. Kate thanked her and noticed that the report was for John Doe 1 and 2. Now, they knew the names of the victims of the fire as Joel Sawyer and Fletcher Potts, both age seventy-eight. Now that positive ID was confirmed, they faced the hardest step: notifying the next of kin.

Kate texted Connor, who was out picking up a warrant on another case. Kate made a copy to put in the file and one for Connor, then set it on his desk. Connor arrived several minutes later. He took off his sport coat and hung it over his chair.

"What's this?" Connor sat and picked up the report.

"Looks like you were right. The bodies were the two elderly men. I wonder where Cole could be."

"No clue. Were you able to get a current photo from Cole's school?"

"Came in yesterday. It's in the file."

"Now we can have the TV and newspapers run it. Ask Sandy to please see if she can get the media to put it out there."

Kate grabbed the photo and headed for Sandy's office.

Connor looked over the report for any helpful information. He spotted an emergency contact on Joel Sawyer's patient information page, obtained with his dental records. However, Joel's emergency contact was his wife, Sylvia. It had never been updated after she passed away. Fletcher's paperwork listed a Jimmy Potts as an emergency contact. Connor quickly checked online and found a J. Potts listed at the address and phone number that Fletcher had listed as belonging to his brother.

Connor, Kate, and Sundae went to the home of Jimmy Potts, Fletcher's younger brother and closest living relative. Before leaving the office, Sandy made Connor and Kate aware of the fact that the brother had been calling every day since the fire to ask if his brother was one of the victims.

Connor knocked on the door. When no one answered, he knocked louder. A moment later, the door was opened by an elderly man in a wheelchair. He rolled the chair back and looked up at them.

"Yes, can I help you?"

"Mr. Potts?" Kate asked.

Connor breathed a sigh of relief that Kate had taken the lead on this. It was just one of the things he felt Kate did better than he did. Connor wasn't quite sure if it was the way she talked to the victims' families or the tone of her voice. Whatever it was, the families just seemed calmer with her.

"I'm Detective Kate Stroup and these are my partners, Detective Connor Maxwell and Sundae, our canine."

"I heard about the fire. I knew it was just a matter of time before someone would let me know. I called the police and fire department every day," Jimmy said as he rolled his wheelchair back from the doorway, allowing the three to enter the living room.

"I'll need to get in touch with a friend to help me make arrangements for Fletcher's funeral now that I know." Jimmy wiped tears from his eyes. "I can't drive and Fletcher…" Jimmy broke down and reached for a tissue on the end table. "Fletcher always drove me when I needed to go somewhere."

"Mr. Potts, we are so sorry for your loss." Kate knelt next to Mr. Potts' wheelchair and gently put her hand on his forearm.

Sundae sat beside the wheelchair and Mr. Potts began petting her. Connor took the opportunity to glance at the photos on the wall. One photo was that of a young twenty-something man in a military uniform, with an equally twenty-something woman standing next to him, smiling. Probably Mr. Potts and possibly Mrs. Potts? Beside it, a photo showed two couples who, Connor guessed, were in their thirties or early forties, sitting around a backyard pool. He sat on the couch.

"Mr. Potts, I know this is a difficult time, but may we talk to you about your brother?" Connor asked.

Mr. Potts blinked back tears and nodded yes.

"Mr. Potts, your brother didn't perish in the fire," Connor began but was interrupted.

"I thought you said…?" Mr. Potts looked

confused and momentarily hoped he had misunderstood what the detectives had said when they had first arrived.

"Mr. Potts, I'm sorry to say that someone shot Fletcher and Mr. Sawyer before setting the house on fire," Kate said.

Jimmy Potts inhaled a large breath, unable to believe what he was hearing.

"Wait, what?" Jimmy shook his head, trying to understand this new information. "My brother, Fletcher Potts, you must have him mixed up with someone else…" Mr. Potts trailed off.

"Both men were shot," Kate said.

Jimmy looked between Kate and Connor. "Shot?"

Connor asked, "Do you know of anyone who would want to harm your brother or Mr. Sawyer?"

"Harm, them? No." Jimmy shook his head. "They're hardly the type to engage in any activity that would bring them into contact with people wanting to hurt either one of them. Detectives, my brother was seventy-eight years old and I believe Joel was either seventy-eight or seventy-nine, I'm not sure. Who would want to…? They golfed together, went to church. Took Joel's son to school. I don't know of anyone who would want to hurt either one of them.

"The news reported that only two bodies were found. You mentioned Joel. What about Joel's adopted son, Cole?" Jimmy asked, reaching for another tissue.

"The news report was correct. We found only two bodies. Dental records identified Joel, and the number on an artificial hip was traced back to your brother. We have no idea where Cole is."

"Cole can't speak," Jimmy said, assuming no one had told the authorities about that.

"Yes, we were made aware of that by another source. The news will start airing Cole's photo today now that we know who the two victims are. Do you know Cole personally?" Connor asked.

"I've met the boy many times. He's a very good kid. Smart, too. Do you think he made it out of the fire and got scared? You know, there's a large forest area right behind the house."

"Yes, we know about the forest. Once we knew that three men were living in the home, we searched the forest but didn't find him." Kate said.

"We've taken up enough of your time. Here are our cards. If you think of anything that might be helpful, please give us a call." Connor laid the business cards on the end table next to several wadded-up tissues.

Kate and Sundae stood to leave with Connor. Kate took Jimmy's hand.

"If there's anything, anything at all we can do, please call us," she said, then walked toward the door.

"Have you told Logan yet?"

"Who?" Connor turned, a confused look on his face.

"Logan is Joel's oldest son," Jimmy said.

"No one told us about Logan. We heard only about Cole," Connor said.

"I'm not surprised," Mr. Potts said.

Connor and Kate turned and sat back down.

"What can you tell us about Logan?" Connor asked.

"I know I shouldn't talk about him after he just lost his father, but Fletcher told me one time, when we were together, without Joel, that Logan was a very angry young man," Jimmy said.

"Did he say why?" Kate asked.

"No, I'm not really sure," Jimmy said.

CHAPTER 5

Connor and Carlos stood beside the hospital bed where Carlos' grandmother lay. She'd had another heart attack. This was the third one and the worst thus far. Tubes and wires ran in all directions as monitors beeped and chimed in the background. Carlos and his beagle, Pebbles, had been staying with Connor and Sundae since Nana had to be rushed to the hospital by ambulance a few days earlier.

"Mi hijo." Nana opened her eyes. "Would you mind getting me some water?"

Carlos reached for the blue plastic pitcher on his grandmother's bedside table.

"No, no, Mi hijo. Take my pitcher and refill it by the nurse's station, please, with ice, too."

Carlos took the pitcher and left the room.

His grandmother extended a frail, shaky hand toward Connor and handed him a small, crumpled piece of paper she had been holding in her hand. Connor took the piece of paper and unfolded it. The handwriting was probably not that of Nana or Carlos, maybe a nurse or a nurse's assistant. It was a name and phone number.

"What is this?" Connor asked.

"If something was to happen to me…" Tears filled her eyes and spilled down her cheeks. She reached out to Connor and placed her hand on his. "You're a good man. Carlos' father died in prison and his mother overdosed on drugs. I'm all he has, except for you."

"You want me to take Carlos?"

"I had my nurse call an attorney yesterday. That is his phone number. If you would take Carlos and give him a home, I know he would love living with you and Sundae." She paused to get a breath. "You have been more of a parent to him than his biological mother or father. Please think about it." Nana patted Connor's hand.

Carlos came rushing back into the room. Connor could hear the ice and water sloshing back and forth in the pitcher. He reached for a small cup from the stack on Nana's tray and carefully filled the cup.

"We'd better go, Carlos. You have school tomorrow and I'm sure Sundae and Pebbles are waiting for dinner," Connor said, putting his hand on the boy's shoulder.

Connor glanced back at Nana and then at Carlos. Connor had met Carlos and his grandmother several years back. He and Sundae had been chasing a suspect the department had been looking for. The subject had hit Sundae over the head, knocked her out, and taken her police identification off her. Carlos had found the beagle lying in an alley. He had carried her home and he and his grandmother had cared for the beagle.

When Connor and Sundae were reunited, it had broken the young boy's heart. With Nana's permission, Connor had gotten Carlos his own beagle. With Nana unable to drive, Connor took Carlos out several times a week on hiking trips, to arcades, for pizza, and to dog training classes, all of which Connor paid for. The two had become best friends.

However, if something were to happen to Nana, Connor could suddenly become an instant parent to the boy. Not by blood, but by choice. Connor wondered if he'd be a good parent to Carlos. When he'd been married before, both Connor and his wife had talked about having children. They never had, thankfully, as the marriage had ended in divorce. Now, if he agreed to this arrangement, he would become an instant, single parent. *How hard could that be?* he thought to himself. He already spent several days a week with Carlos and the boy had even spent the night a few times. They got along well, but would this new dynamic change that?

"You wanted to go." Carlos tugged on Connor's arm, bringing him out of his thoughts.

Connor flushed with embarrassment that his thoughts had drifted so far.

"You're right, Carlos. We'd better be going. Nana, you get better," Connor said.

Nana smiled at him. "You think about it, please," she said as they walked out of the room.

That evening, Connor took stock of his home. What would he have to change? When Carlos stayed over, he slept in a makeshift guest room, bringing a small duffle bag from his home. Living at Connor's house permanently meant that Carlos would need a place for all his belongings, not just a few changes of clothes. Connor realized that if this were to be a full-time arrangement, he would have to clean out all the junk that he had shuffled into that room. He would need to buy a better bed, plus a chest of drawers, maybe a bookcase or small desk. Clean out the closet. After a few minutes, Connor was overwhelmed. Nevertheless, he had a lot to think about. He thought a good start would be to let Carlos pick out his own bed and furniture.

"Hey, buddy, what do you think about going out tonight for dinner and after that swinging by a store to get a better bed for you?"

Carlos thought for a minute, as if attempting to wrap his eight-year-old mind around why he needed a better bed. However, if Connor wanted a better bed in the guestroom, he'd go along with it.

"Cool. Can Kate come, too?"

"I don't know if she has plans or not. Give her a call and see," Connor said as he handed Carlos his cell phone.

---

After dinner, Connor, Kate, and Carlos stopped by a furniture store off Main Street. Carlos checked out all the twin-size beds, lying on them and pretending he was asleep until Kate laughed. Then he scampered off to the next one.

"So, are you going to tell me what's going on here?" Kate asked once Carlos was out of earshot.

"Nana called an attorney. She wants me to adopt Carlos if something happens to her."

Kate stopped walking and turned toward Connor but said nothing. Connor stopped and looked at Kate.

"What? You don't think I could be a good dad?"

"Given the parents the poor kid had, I'd think he hit the dad lottery," Kate said, putting her arm around Connor's waist.

CHAPTER 6

Logan Sawyer went to the Lakewood Police Department at the department's request. Kate and Connor observed him through the one-way glass in the hallway. He sat by himself in the small interview room, which was nicknamed the box. He appeared to be around six feet tall—maybe six-three by the look of his long legs, which stretched out to the side of the table. He had a dark complexion with dark features. He fiddled with his phone, then shoved it back into his pants pocket. Kate figured him for a ladies' man. At least, he had the tall, dark, and handsome thing going for him.

Logan's behavior of shaking his head, looking at his watch every few seconds, and sighing dramatically showed his irritation. Connor assumed that was because he'd been asked to come in to answer some questions.

Connor, Kate, and Sundae entered the box and took their places across from Logan.

"Mr. Sawyer, I'm Detective Maxwell and this is my partner, Detective Stroup," Connor said as Kate slid their business cards across the table.

He glanced at the two cards for a second. "What? The mutt doesn't have a business card?" Logan asked sarcastically, ignoring the cards in front of him.

Neither Connor nor Kate responded.

"Look, I'm a busy man. Can we cut all the formalities and get on with this dog," Logan looked under the table at Sundae, "and pony show?"

"Mr. Sawyer, we're sorry for the loss of your father, not to mention, your brother is missing," Kate said. "I can't imagine how…" Kate was cut off mid-sentence.

"B-r-o-t-h-e-r? You do know I don't have a biological brother, don't you?" Logan seemed appalled to be referred to as Cole's older brother. "I assume you're meaning Cole, whom my late mother and father took in. But thank you for the sentiment for my father."

Connor watched Logan's body language closely

as Kate continued her questioning. *Something is off*, Connor thought to himself. Logan simply didn't act like a man who had just lost his father.

"I'm sorry. We were under the impression that your father and mother had adopted Cole when he was just a child, which would make you his brother," Kate said, knowing that the Sawyers had adopted the boy.

"Yeah, sure. They adopted the little retard but that doesn't make him my brother," Logan blurted out.

Kate looked over at Connor before continuing. "I take it you and Cole don't get along?"

"He was okay at first. Then everything was Cole this and Cole that ... Cole had to get the best of everything, go to the best schools and university. You just get tired of that after a while, you know?"

"Do you have any idea where your brother—I mean, Cole—might be?"

"Honestly, when I heard about the fire, I figured the little punk burnt up in the blaze," Logan said, pulling a piece of dead skin from his thumb.

"So, you heard about the fire. May I ask how?" asked Kate.

"On TV. That reporter with the big boobs,

Candy Martin, did a report on it the night it happened."

"Did you contact the Lakewood Police Department after you heard about the fire?"

"No."

Kate looked over at Connor, knowing that dispatch had said the only family member who had called was Fletcher's brother.

"The fire department?"

"No. They said two men burned in the fire. I assumed there was no reason to contact them. It had to be my father." Logan tipped his chair back on two legs and folded his arms across his chest.

"Did you go by the house after the fire?"

"No."

"May I ask, how did you find out that one of the victims was your father?"

"His dentist's office called me. They thought I already knew, so that's how I heard, okay?"

"I'm sorry you had to hear about it that way. When we questioned your father's neighbors, they mentioned a son, but we assumed they were talking about Cole."

"Look, I need to be going ... if there isn't anything else," Logan stood up and pushed the chair away. "I'll let myself out."

"Actually, there is, Mr. Sawyer," Connor said, standing to block the doorway. "Where were you on the night of the fire?"

"Go to hell, Detective. If you want me to answer any more questions, you can contact my attorney." Logan pushed by Connor and left the room.

"That young man has a very large chip on his shoulder," Kate said.

"He mentioned he thought Cole burnt the place up. I wonder what he based that on," Connor said.

"He sounds as though he could be very jealous about the affection his mother and father showed Cole," Kate said.

---

A call came in on the tip hotline that a young boy matching Cole Sawyer's description had been seen. The boy had been hanging around outside of Dan's, a small mom-and-pop coffee and pastry store, looking for discarded food.

"Detective, I saw his photo on TV. I'm sure he was the young man you're looking for. His one pant leg looked like it was burnt and he had an open wound on that leg."

"You're sure his pant leg was burnt?" Connor asked.

"I took him a croissant and a cup of hot coffee when we saw him going through our trash can out front." Dan motioned to a wire mesh trash can outside. "When I called to him, he wouldn't take it from me, so I set it down on the table out front. I told him to take it. His clothes still smelled like smoke," Dan said.

"Did he eat out there or take it and leave?" Connor asked.

"Honestly, he grabbed the food and ran toward the forest over there. I yelled out and told him that if he came back tomorrow, I'd give him more. He looked hungry."

"Did he speak at all to you?" Connor asked.

"Not a word."

Connor, Kate, and Sundae walked toward the forest area where Dan had indicated. They hiked into the forest, hoping to see at least the plate or cup discarded on the forest floor. However, they found nothing but a bed of pine needles and branches. Sundae, being tri-colored, almost blended in with the fall forest color. If it hadn't been for the white tip of her tail, they would have lost sight of her at times. After about an hour's walk into the forest, they turned back and returned to Dan's Coffee and Pastry Shop, where they made plans to be inside the next morning to see if Cole would return.

The following morning Connor, Kate, and Sundae sat inside, waiting to see if Cole would show up. Kate sipped a chocolate mocha latte and nibbled a second cream cheese scone. As Connor finished his pumpkin spice latte, he saw a young man walk out of the forest. One leg of his jeans was either torn or burnt up to his knee. Connor pointed him out to Kate.

"Let him get closer," Connor said.

They sat and watched the person whom they believed to be Cole Sawyer walking toward Dan's Coffee and Pastry Shop.

"Do you want me to take him something?" Dan asked.

"No, let him get close to the trash can," Connor said.

The boy reached into the trash can, where Connor had placed a wrapped pumpkin scone. As Cole carefully examined the scone, Connor walked out the front door.

"Cole, Cole Sawyer," Connor said.

The young man bolted toward the forest as Kate and Sundae ran out of Dan's.

CHAPTER 7

"Give chase, do not take down," Connor commanded Sundae. He ran across the street behind Sundae, who was now about ten feet away from Cole, while Connor was about fifteen feet behind. *God, this kid is fast for having an injured leg.* Connor had misjudged him. He remembered thinking to himself that catching the kid would be easy. Boy, had he underestimated him!

Cole ran into a thicket, jumping high over thick dead branches and through dense trees. He looked over his left shoulder, and then his right as he put more distance between himself and Connor. Sundae tried to jump into the thicket only to get hung up on the tangle of branches. She yelped in pain as the brush poked into her skin. Sundae struggled to get out. When she finally broke free, she turned and bolted several feet to the right, then back to the left, searching franticly for a way around the thicket. Connor jumped into the thicket as Kate caught up to Sundae.

"Stay," Kate commanded Sundae.

While she could see that the beagle was too small to get through the dense brush, Kate heard the sound of snapping branches and leaves under Connor's feet.

Connor saw a piece of Cole's shirt that had snagged onto a branch and grabbed it while never breaking his stride. He put it in his sport coat pocket.

"Cole, wait, please!" Connor yelled out.

Cole hesitated for a second, looked at Connor, then continued to run. He glanced back over his shoulder again. This time, he tripped over a fallen tree trunk. With Connor about twelve feet away, Cole quickly got to his feet, jumped over the tree trunk, and took off at a dead run. Connor jumped over the tree and kept gaining on Cole.

Cole's mind flashed back to when he was a young child. Memories returned of his foster dad chasing him after the woman had burnt him. No longer did he see Connor. Rather, he imagined that the foster father was running after him. Cole had to run as fast as he could to get away from these people. If the man caught him, they would harm him again and again. The burn on his lower leg had hurt but now it was screaming in pain. In Cole's mind, the injury wasn't from the fire that had taken the life of his adopted dad. It was from the foster parents he'd had when he was a young child. They had burned him for wetting the bed, put him in their basement, naked and cold, without food for three days. To Cole, this was not the voice of Connor Maxwell. It was a voice that echoed from his past: the foster father.

"Cole!" Connor called out again.

A branch tore the upper arm of Connor's sport coat, ripping through the fabric of both the jacket and his shirt and tearing into his flesh.

"Son of a bitch!" Connor yelled out in pain.

Cole heard the language and remembered hearing the same tone and verbiage from his foster father. Turning back, he could no longer see the man chasing him. That didn't stop him. He kept up the pace, putting more distance between them.

Connor felt something catch his left leg. He had

been running and his momentum caused him to tumble down into a large ditch like a sack of degraded trash. He rolled until his upper body crashed down face-first onto the forest floor. His left ankle was wedged between two tree trunks. Connor sat upright in pain. He tried pushing and pulling the tree trunks but failed. Two squirrels barked from high above him.

"Sure, easy for you to say," he said to the squirrels.

He then pulled on his leg with great force, trying to remove his foot from his boot. Finally, his foot came out, leaving his sock in the boot. With his foot out, Connor worked the leather boot free and quickly put his sock and boot back on. Standing upright, he brushed himself off and tried to assess the time lost. Could he still catch up to the kid? He looked at his wristwatch but had no idea how long it had taken to free himself. Connor stood with his eyes closed, listening. He heard nothing except the screech of a red-tailed hawk overhead. Connor turned and walked back to the thicket where Kate and Sundae waited. *Why was the kid running away? Unless he's guilty.* Connor limped over to Kate.

"Connor, your arm is bleeding bad," Kate said, checking the wound. "I think you need stitches. And what happened to your leg?" Kate brushed pine needles from his coat.

"I hit two trees at about ninety miles per hour." Connor chuckled and held out the piece of torn cloth from Cole's shirt. "We need a piece of this for Sundae. The rest we'll send over to our CSI team."

"Could you see where he's been hiding?"

"No, he just kept running. I called out, but that just made him run faster."

They walked back to Dan's Coffee and Pastry Shop.

"I know you think he set the fire but what if the fire tripped something in his mind ... a memory from his past?" Kate asked.

"I don't know. Why run if you're not guilty?"

"Why don't we ask Beth? She's the resident head doctor for the department."

"Can't hurt," Connor said as he opened Kate's door, then Sundae's.

Dan poked his head out of the store's front door. "Any luck?" he asked.

"No," Connor replied.

Beth Ellis had worked for the FBI's Behavioral Science Unit for several years before going out on her own and consulting for law enforcement agencies. She was an elegant woman with impeccable looks.

"Beth, I told Connor that Cole might be running away from him because of something in his past and not the fire," Kate said.

Beth had a copy of Cole's records in her lap. She had marked the copy with several colored page flags. "It's quite possible that the fire at the house was what we call a trigger." Beth paused, turning to a page of Cole's records. "As a small child, he was burned for wetting his bed. Authorities later discovered the foster parents had locked him in their basement, naked, without blankets to keep him warm. Three days with no food. So yes, this could trigger the young man to relive that part of his childhood."

"But I'm not his foster parent," Connor said.

Beth thought for a moment before she continued. "I want to explain. If this theory is correct, Cole will look at Connor and see the foster father and you," she looked over at Kate, "as the foster mother." Beth tapped her pen on her pad.

"If that's the case, no adult male or female can approach him?" Connor asked.

"I'd like to meet with Fletcher Potts' brother. From what you told me, the older son, Logan Sawyer, and Cole didn't get along. I'm hoping that Fletcher's brother may recall how Joel and his wife were able to deal and eventually get through to Cole when he first moved in with the Sawyers. Again, this may be a reach, and Fletcher's brother may not know. The other thing is that Cole stayed in the state boy's home for a time and it's possible that the Sawyers didn't have to deal with this trigger. However, I would bet money they did. Nonetheless, it's worth us going over there."

"Is there anything else from his records that would help us?" Connor asked.

"If there is any way you could search the forest again, I would wager a guess that wherever Cole is bedding down for the night, he's having night terrors. This may or may not have him wetting his clothes during the night. Sundae should be able to pick up on the smell of urine. If he's gone from the area, leave food and a note explaining who you are and stating that you only want to help. Don't put the items too close to where he is staying—just close enough for him to find. It may take several tries before you're able to get close enough to him," Beth suggested.

Kate and Connor agreed and set up a meeting with Jimmy Potts. Then they went shopping. They purchased bottled water, two coolers, packages of food, blankets, a pencil, a pen, and a pad of paper in case Cole wanted to leave them a note. Kate picked out a heavy flannel shirt and jeans that she thought might fit Cole, along with heavy socks. When they had last seen him, Cole had been wearing only torn jeans and a tee shirt. Connor grabbed a backpack into which they could put everything. Next, Connor drove to a large chain bookstore to look for advanced math puzzle books. They picked out two. Before they left, Connor chose a math puzzle book for Carlos' age group and purchased it as well.

Kate laughed. "And you're worried whether you'd make a good dad for Carlos."

Connor chose to ignore her comment.

With the temperature dropping, Connor ran by a sporting goods store and purchased a sleeping bag and battery-operated lantern. He also grabbed two Moultrie battery-operated trail cams from the shelf. He examined the package, making sure the model had an SD card and batteries.

Their last stop was the drug store. Kate purchased bandages and an over-the-counter antibiotic ointment for Cole to put on his leg wound. Together, they decided that Kate should write the letter to Cole. Tomorrow, they would return to the forest and see if they could find where Cole might be staying.

CHAPTER 8

The following morning, Connor turned on the TV before he left for work, paying particular attention to the weather report. The weatherman was a colorful man who always wore a brightly colored bowtie and, oftentimes, matching suspenders. Connor assumed Mrs. Weatherman must have quite the knack for finding matching bowties and suspenders. Today, the weatherman was mismatched, wearing a bright orange bowtie with white polka dots and bright blue suspenders. At this hour in the morning, the contrast against his white shirt made Connor back away from the TV a bit. What Connor really needed was the weather report. Mr. Suspenders, as

Connor called him, was calling for snow in the high country and a drop in the temperatures.

Connor reviewed the list of supplies for Cole and decided to grab a few things from his own camping gear, then stop by the sporting goods store before he picked up Kate. He would purchase a small tent, foot and hand warmers, and more blankets. He decided to take his own four-wheel SUV and leave his unmarked police unit at home, just in case the weather forecast was spot on.

He dropped off Carlos at school and purchased the tent and other supplies, then drove to Kate's house. As she opened the SUV door, the interior filled with the aroma of freshly baked cookies.

"I smell cookies!" Connor said as he began going through the bags Kate set between them.

"Hey, you stay out of those," Kate said, smiling and swatting Connor's hand. "Those are for Cole!"

Connor put on his most hurt, bad-boy look, then smiled as he backed out of her driveway.

"Okay, one. That's all you get!" Kate relented. She handed him a cholate chip cookie and brushed the unruly lock of hair from his forehead. *God, he's so damn good-looking*, she thought to herself. Then she reminded herself to be professional.

"I went back to the sporting goods store and

picked up a tent for Cole this morning. Mr. Suspenders, aka the weatherman, said temps will drop and we could get snow in the high country," Connor said.

They drove out to Dan's Coffee and Pastry Shop, where they would carry everything as far as they could for Cole to hopefully find and put to use.

"On my way home yesterday afternoon, I picked up a forestry service map." Kate showed the map to Connor. "I also ran by a store and got these gloves for his hands. Oh, and I called Dan at the coffee shop to let him know that, in my letter to Cole, I told him to go to Dan's and that Dan would call us for him, no questions asked," Kate said.

"Okay. Let me get this straight. You laughed at me yesterday for buying Carlos a math book. Last night or this morning, you baked homemade cookies and got gloves for Cole," Connor said, smiling.

"What?" Kate said.

"Nothing. By the way, you'll make a great mom someday," Connor said.

Kate reached over and punched his arm.

Kate, Connor, and Sundae hiked up into the forest, finding a safe way around the thicket. Beyond that, they found where Cole had left the empty coffee cup from Dan's next to a tree. Sundae sniffed around the area but didn't alert them.

"Maybe he just stopped here that day to drink the coffee and eat the pastry," Connor said, walking beyond the area.

Kate and Sundae followed. Connor could feel the temperature dropping, just as Mr. Suspenders had promised. He stopped and pulled out Sundae's dark blue coat, which said "Police K9" on each side. Kate took the opportunity to wrap her scarf tightly around her neck and pull out a stocking cap.

Kate looked around. "We'd better not go too far. Beth said that way we wouldn't send him into fight-or-flight mode."

"This is beyond where I was yesterday. I would've remembered seeing the empty coffee cup. I'll put the first trail cam here."

Connor looked around for the best tree for the camera. Once he found the tree, he strapped the camera around the tree trunk.

"I have it set to alert me on my cell phone when the camera detects any motion."

With the SD card already inserted, Connor opened the waterproof flap and turned the camera on.

"Walk in front of the camera. I need to test it."

Within a few seconds, Connor heard his phone chime. He pulled out the phone and saw a photo of Kate walking in front of the tree. He showed her the photo.

"Will it be able to take photos at night?" Kate asked.

"Sure will, only they'll be in black and white, not color like your photo."

Connor gathered up the supplies and they walked higher into the forest. Sundae suddenly sat and howled, alerting them. Connor quickly released her so that she would stop howling. He didn't want her to spook Cole if he was in the area. Connor surveyed the area. There was a depression in the pine needles that looked like someone had bedded down in it. They found food wrappers—maybe from something Cole had purchased but more likely from a trash bin.

"Let's back down this trail a few feet and set up everything for him," Connor said.

They went about fifteen feet back down the trail. Connor positioned the two small coolers, one of which contained fresh water. He put the food in the other cooler and snapped the clasp shut. Then he set up the tent and placed the backpack inside it. Kate taped a sign with Coles' name on the tent. She hoped that he would understand that the tent and supplies were for him to use and were not someone else's camp. Kate's letter was in the backpack. It was midafternoon before everything was in place and they had set up the second trail cam.

It was now time to head back down the mountain. Connor covered everything they had left outside the tent with a blue plastic tarp and weighted down the four corners. Sundae had made herself at home inside the tent and was fast asleep. Snow the size of popcorn began to flutter down, slowly at first but quickly accelerating.

"Let's go," Connor said, waking up Sundae.

As they made their way through the trees, Sundae ran in front but looked around to make sure Connor and Kate were behind her.

"I'm worried about him," Kate said as she pulled her gloves from her coat pocket.

"Kate, I have a tarp over the tent. I have a tarp over the other supplies. I put two wool blankets under the sleeping bag so that it's elevated off the ground. It's not five-star accommodations but he can survive as long as he comes back there and makes use of the things, we brought him."

"But where is he?" Kate asked with a motherly worried tone.

"Kate, calm down. For all we know, he may have been watching us," Connor said, taking her by the arm as they started to hike back to his SUV. The snow began falling faster.

"Mr. Suspenders sure nailed this forecast," Connor said.

The snow was coming down so hard, it was difficult to see their hands in front of them. It would be easy to get turned around in these hills. Kate pulled her coat tighter around her. Connor could tell that she was worried about Cole staying up there by himself in this blizzard. The trail before them was imposing and increasingly difficult to navigate with the large roots and rocks now completely covered in snow. Kate took several steps, then began to slip on a large snow-covered rock, losing her footing. Connor quickly grabbed her. They both stopped.

"You okay?"

"Yes, but I thought we passed this tree a few minutes ago."

Kate turned around three hundred and sixty degrees.

CHAPTER 9

Connor studied their surroundings. He had to admit that Kate was right in at least one aspect. The forest, when covered in a fresh white blanket of snow, all looked the same. To avoid worrying her, he waited until she was looking the other way, then snapped a branch just enough so that it dangled. That way, he would know if they had passed the area before. Looking back in the direction from which they had just come, he could see that the snow had already covered their tracks.

The mountain breeze was now a blizzard swirling the snow around them. Based on the slope, Connor's gut feeling told him that they were descending the mountain. But which side? Connor had hiked mountains all his life and he knew all too well how low visibility could turn people around. Even pilots had been known to turn their light aircraft upside down and fly directly into the side of a mountain in snow.

While they were stopped, Connor used the opportunity to pull a set of insulated snow boots for Sundae out of his backpack. He brushed the snow from one paw and put the first boot on her foot. The boots were not only insulated and waterproof but also provided a good anti-slip molded rubber sole for the beagle. He repeated the process for each paw. While Sundae did not like wearing her snow boots, he knew that she needed protection from the cold just as much as they did. He then brushed the snow from her winter coat. Before hoisting his backpack onto his shoulders, Connor offered Kate and Sundae what was left of their water. Kate took a small sip, though Sundae refused. He tucked the water bottle into a mesh pocket inside his backpack, close to his body, so that it wouldn't freeze. Then Connor pulled on his backpack and the three began carefully walking downhill again.

After another fifteen minutes of their slow descent, inching their way down the mountainside, Connor's feet were getting cold, even with his waterproof hiking boots. The toes on both his feet were getting numb. He knew, without even asking, that Kate's feet had to be cold as well. The frigid air sent shards of pain into his lungs, making them feel as though they were on fire with each breath. Connor pulled the collar of his coat around his mouth and tucked his nose inside the collar flap. He pulled off his baseball cap and shook the snow off it. The stubble on his face was beyond hope, as it was now frozen. In the sky, the sun behind the snow filled clouds had begun its descent into the horizon.

Part of him wanted to go back to the campsite they had set up for Cole and wait out the storm. However, he knew that Cole would need all the protection they had left him. When Connor had chased the young man in the forest yesterday, all he had been wearing were jeans, sneakers, and a tee shirt. He assumed that was probably all that Cole had been wearing on the night of the fire, which was not much protection from the cold and wind. Connor looked at his watch. They'd been hiking down the slippery face of the mountain for a little over an hour.

He wanted to pull his cellphone out of his jacket pocket and check the compass app but he didn't want to alarm Kate. Instead, he told her that he wanted to check the trail cam app. Once he got out the phone, he quickly checked the compass app. Connor breathed a sigh of relief when he saw that they were going in the correct direction. He knew they had to veer off to the east before the thicket. Then back to the north. Before he put away his phone, he noticed that his battery was at fifteen percent, most likely from the cold. He unzipped his coat and put the phone in the inside pocket, close to his chest, for body heat. Then he thought to himself, *What body heat in this weather, right?*

"How much battery do you have left? Connor asked Kate.

She pulled her phone from her pocket. "Only twenty percent. I charged it last night."

"Put it in the inside pocket of your coat to keep it warmer."

Kate did as Connor suggested. Connor reached down and picked up Sundae to give her a break from the cold. He took Kate by the arm and began walking down a steep hill. They did more sliding than walking. Each slip caused Kate to shriek until Connor was able to stop her. The snow on the face of the mountain piled higher. Kate pulled her scarf more tightly around her neck and face. Connor could feel Kate shivering violently against the cold as he held her arm tightly. Sundae was shivering, too. They stopped once again so that Connor could pull his leather belt from his pants. He put it around the lower outside part of his coat and pulled it tight. Unzipping his coat, he tucked Sundae inside so that only her face was exposed to the cold and she could tuck her head inside his jacket if she wanted to. The leather belt provided a stop so that Sundae wouldn't slip down and out of his coat. The belt also prevented the cold air from entering the coat. However, this setup now exposed Connor's face and lungs to the cold. Every few steps, he put his face down to Sundae for warmth. Kate wanted to stop every couple of yards.

"I can't feel my feet anymore. Can't we just stop for a rest?" Kate pleaded.

"We've gone around the thicket. We have only a few more..." Connor said, as she shook her head no.

"Jump up on my back. I'll carry you the rest of the way." Connor turned his back to her.

"Connor, you can't carry us both in this snow."

"Jump up, take the backpack put it on" he commanded.

His hands were so cold, he almost failed to lift her. Once in place, he carefully walked through the snow. The mountain terrain was leveling out now.

Connor was beginning to feel warm all over; he wasn't sure if it was due to Sundae's and Kate's body heat next to him or if hyperthermia was setting in. He knew that people exposed to the cold for too long had a sensation of heat.

He had to keep moving and keep his blood flowing to get the three of them off this godforsaken frozen tundra. He willed himself to take one step after another. His body was exhausted. Maybe Kate was right. A short rest would help. However, he knew that would take up valuable time. They would just grow more tired, to the point that they would fall asleep and slip into the doorway of death.

CHAPTER 10

Connor felt the fatigue in his legs, back, and arms. Several times, he thought his knees would buckle, sending the three of them sliding down the mountain ass over teakettles. He didn't know how long he had carried Kate on his back and Sundae tucked into his coat. His mind attempted a guess but he had no idea. All he could think of was getting off this damn mountain alive. The snow was a white wall falling at a slant, and the wind blew so hard that Connor almost lost his balance and fell backward several times. The temperature had continued to drop. Connor thought to himself that even Frosty the Snowman and Santa would rethink coming out in weather like this.

He wanted to take his mind off the cold and

wind, so he thought of the case they were working on, the fire and homicide at 2255 Decker Avenue. He had asked Detectives Bob Barton and Grant Harris to keep an eye on Logan Sawyer while Connor and Kate were gone. Kate felt certain that Cole had nothing to do with the murder and fire that had taken the lives of his adopted father, Joel Sawyer, and his friend, Fletcher Potts. Connor mulled over all the facts and his interview with Logan Sawyer. Could Logan's attitude be a simple case of sibling rivalry and jealousy over the fact that his late mother and father had adopted Cole? Worse yet, could that be a wedge that would have led him to shoot his own father and Fletcher in the back of the head, then set fire to the home in an effort to cover up the murder? If that was the case, how had Cole managed to get away from Logan and escape the fire with only a burn on his lower leg?

The smell of food brought Connor out of his thoughts. Could they be getting closer to Dan's? Or was his mind playing tricks on him? Then he saw a flicker of light through the snow and trees. It had to be the street light by Dan's parking lot.

"Kate, I'm going to set you down. Do you think you can walk the rest of the way? I think I can see Dan's."

Kate had been dosing off as she rode on Connor's back. The front half of her body had been kept warm next to his body. His voice sounded raspy as he woke her up. She wondered how long it had taken them to travel down the face of the mountain.

"I'll try."

Connor carefully set her down. Even with gloves, his fingers were so cold that they refused to straighten out. They had held Kate's legs in one position so long that his bones felt as though they were welded fast in a half-curled posture.

"Over there, can you see the light from the parking lot?" Connor tried to point in the direction of the light. When his finger refused to cooperate, he thrust his fist in the direction.

Kate looked to where Connor was pointing. and saw the light.

"We made it!" she yelled.

Connor pulled Kate toward the light. As they got closer, Connor could make out the red neon sign that hung in Dan's window. The smell of food filled the night air as they emerged from the forest and crossed the snow-covered street. Turning back, Connor looked up at the mountain. What had almost claimed their lives now looked like a winter wonderland straight off a Christmas card.

"I'd run if I could," Kate said.

"I could use a cup of hot coffee. How about you?" Connor asked.

Kate simply nodded. Connor got Sundae out of his coat. She scampered around in the snow, then started to roll in it, in an attempt to remove her coat.

"You keep that on until we get inside Dan's," Connor commanded. Sundae got up and ran happily in circles around Connor and Kate.

"Glad one of us feels like running," Connor said and laughed.

---

Connor held the door open for Kate. The warmth and aroma wafted out the door and greeted them. He looked up to the heavens and said a silent "thank you" to God for getting them out alive.

"Oh, my word!" Dan said, hurrying from behind the pastry counter to meet them. "I was going to call your department in another hour if you hadn't returned. Now I wish I would have called earlier."

He ushered them to a table next to the fireplace. "Kate, do you want your regular chocolate latte? And Connor, do you want pumpkin?"

"Yes," Connor, said still rubbing his hands together.

Dan left and returned several minutes later with two large, steaming lattes.

"Kate, would you please take off Sundae's coat?" Connor asked. "You can leave her boots on." He was still unable to use his hands other than to wrap them around the cup of hot coffee.

"I have warm pastries coming out in a few minutes," Dan said as he smoothed down his black apron and turned back to the kitchen.

"I feel so guilty having a hot coffee while Cole is out in that cold forest with nothing warm," Kate said.

Connor reached over and placed his hand on hers. His fingers were starting to warm.

"Kate, I took my one-burner Colman stove up there with three bottles of gas. In the sack I tied to my backpack, I put my camping coffee pot, some coffee, and a small pan. I also put in a hand can opener and several cans of soup, beans, and hot chocolate mix. As long as Cole finds all that stuff we left before Yogi the Bear does, he'll be just fine."

Dan returned to their table carrying a plate stacked high with his famous cream cheese croissants.

"Yum," Kate said, reaching for the top pastry.

"I'll bring a bowl of water out for Ms. Sundae. May I bring her anything to eat?" Dan asked.

"Water would be great. I have some food for her in my truck." Connor started to get up.

"No, you sit. I'll go get it. It's the least I can do," Kate said. She turned to Dan. "Did you know that Connor carried me and Sundae down the mountain?"

Dan just shook his head. "May I get you both more coffee?"

"That would be great," Connor said.

For the first time since entering Dan's, Connor unzipped his coat. Kate returned with Sundae's small travel bowl and kibble, which Sundae gobbled up. Then Sundae laid down at Connor's feet.

Connor's phone dinged. He pulled it out of his chest pocket. He could see that the trail cam had captured an image. Just as he clicked to view it, his battery died.

CHAPTER 11

"Is your charger in your truck? I'll go get it." Kate stood up and started for the door.

"Wait, no. It's in the police unit at home, and yours won't work. Finish eating and I'll get the bill. Then we can head over to my place."

Connor looked at his watch. "I need to let Carlos' sitter go home, too. That way, we can see what we have on the trail cam. You can take my unit home and pick me up in the morning," he said as he sipped his coffee and took the last bite of his croissant

Beth Ellis waited in the lobby of the police department for an officer to escort her. It was a department rule that a consultant hired by the Lakewood Police Department had to be accompanied by an officer to a residence. Beth herself had once been an FBI agent, but rules were rules. Detectives Barton and Harris were to accompany Beth to Jimmy Potts' house. However, they were following Logan Sawyer into a seedy area of Lakewood, so they radioed in to dispatch and asked for an officer to accompany Beth. She wanted to ask for any input on how Mr. and Mrs. Sawyer had been able to deal with Cole's triggers. Beth felt that Cole must have had them when he first moved in with them. However, had the Sawyers conveyed that information to Fletcher and then possibly on to Jimmy? That remained to be seen. Jimmy was the younger brother of Fletcher Potts, who had been shot and left in the burning house

The lobby door opened and a petite, bouncy female uniformed officer with shoulder-length brown hair walked toward Beth.

"You must be Beth Ellis," Officer Jackie Martinez said, extending her hand.

"Glad to meet you, Officer Martinez," Beth said, shaking Jackie's hand. She was anxious to get her interview going and see if she could learn any information for Connor's investigation.

"Detective Barton gave me the address I need to take you to. Are you ready?"

Beth nodded, picked up her briefcase, and followed the officer.

---

Logan Sawyer parked his BMW i8 Coupe, pearl white with blue accents, in a strip mall parking lot, then began walking behind a row of buildings. Bob rolled ever so slowly by the alley and Grant got out. He was on foot to see where Logan was going.

Bob retraced their path back by the BMW. In this neighborhood, Logan's car stood out like a side of beef at a vegan fest. Bob stepped out and looked through the windows. Ninety to over a hundred thousand, he mused to himself regarding the price of the car. Expensive taste...Whatever the cost, he knew he would never be able to afford a car like this on his detective pay, even with Bettie Jo, his wife, working for the bank. Even if they could afford it, why would they ever waste their money on a fancy luxury car like that? Bob got back into his unit and doubled back to the alley, where

Harris was standing with one foot up against the building.

"Anything?" Bob asked as Grant got into the unit.

"He walked into the back door of a smoke shop." Grant pointed to a red door about halfway down the alley. "I didn't want to blow our cover so I walked by, got the name off the door, and came back here."

Bob looked around and noticed a line of trees parallel to the alley. Behind the tree line was a city park. He pulled the unit out onto the street, hooked around, and then drove into the parking lot, where he threw the car into park.

"Let's go."

Bob and Grant got out of the car and headed toward the line of trees. After standing there for twenty minutes, they were about ready to leave when Logan came out of the smoke shop. He walked past the smoke shop's door and fished something out of his pocket. Quickly, he looked about, making sure no one was around. Then he squatted down with his back against the cinderblock wall, lit up, and began to get high. Grant started through the trees but Bob grabbed his shoulder, shaking his head no.

"Let it go," Bob whispered as he took out his cell phone and snapped a few photos of Logan.

After Logan got his fix, he stood up and walked back to his car, all the while scratching his arms and neck.

"Meth head?" Grant asked Bob.

"That would be my guess."

Bob motioned for them to go back to their car.

"That would explain his short fuse that Connor mentioned," Grant said.

---

After Connor charged his cell phone, he and Kate looked through the trail cam images. They were mostly snow-clad photos. However, in one shot they could see Cole looking inside the tent.

Connor sent a text to Beth, Bob, Grant, and Kate, asking them to meet in the morning to brainstorm their next steps. He heard Kate's cell phone chime with his text and looked over. She had fallen asleep on his couch. After the day they had both endured, the only things that Kate needed to drift off to sleep were a warm bowl of soup, a warm house, and Sundae curled up next to her.

Connor got a pillow from his bedroom and two

blankets. Careful not to wake her, he placed the blankets over Kate, then gently lifted her head onto the pillow and turned out the living room light. He walked down the hallway and quietly opened Carlos' bedroom door. Inside, he saw Pebbles curled into a ball next to Carlos. He stood there, looking at Carlos sound asleep. The room looked better, Connor thought. It looked like a bedroom now. Carlos had an actual place for his clothes in the closet, dresser, and chest of drawers. Connor had even sprung for a small wooden desk, which sat in the corner of the room for Carlos to do his homework. He could see Carlos' backpack hanging from the back of the desk chair. Connor smiled as he closed the door and headed toward his own bedroom.

The following morning, Connor's cell phone contained several photos of Cole. The snow had stopped and the images were much clearer now. The meeting between all the detectives and Beth Ellis started. Bob began.

"We followed Logan around for the better part of the day yesterday. The last place he went before he returned home was a smoke shop out on State Road 10. You know that strip mall?

Connor, Kate, and Beth nodded.

"Grant tailed him on foot until he went inside. We then parked over at the park and hid in the trees, where we watched the dude get high.

"Pot?" Connor asked.

"No. Meth, I'm sure.

"He has expensive taste. The car we tailed was a pearl white BMW i8 Coupe. When we ran the temp tags, it came back to Logan Sawyer. Last night, when I got home, Bettie Jo and I googled it. Those things cost $147,500. This morning, before our meeting, Grant and I went into the BMW dealer. We told them Logan Sawyer had referred us and said that they would make me a good deal on one like his. The salesman told me that Logan was a very nervous man while there. He couldn't tell me any more than that due to privacy issues."

"So, did you take a test drive?" Kate asked, smiling at Bob.

"Yes, they forced me to," Bob said as everyone in the room laughed.

---

Every time he dozed off to sleep, Cole wrestled with his demons and ghosts from the past and present. The letter from the woman had explained that she and the man who had chased him only wanted to help him. But his foster parents had chased him, only to lock him in the basement naked and cold without food.

Cole sat up shaking, not from the cold but from a nightmare. This time, it was the one where he heard two loud pops. He got out of bed and the house was on fire. He remembered seeing Joel and Fletcher through the flames on the floor, bleeding. He had tried several times to reach them when his pants caught on fire and the flames burnt his lower leg. He always woke up at that point. Were Joel and Fletcher, okay? He took the pen and writing tablet they'd left him and wrote, "I love you, Dad," as tears fell from his eyes.

He laid back, thinking about what he should do. Could he trust the man and the woman? He just wanted to go home, home to Joel and Fletcher. He had gone back to the house the day after the fire but the house was gone. Where would he live? His thoughts were interrupted when he heard a loud growl and saw the shadow of a bear on the tent.

CHAPTER 12

Beth shuffled through the notes sitting on the lap of her midnight blue pencil skirt as Detective Barton finished relaying all the intel he and Harris had gathered on Logan Sawyer. Kate watched Beth, wondering where the woman purchased her sophisticated business suits. Beth's jewelry and clothes always had an elegant air to them. Kate mused to herself that Beth had probably never worn a pair of sweatpants in her life. Nevertheless, Beth's taste in attire was beyond what Kate could afford. She wondered if Beth would consider passing down her outfits to Kate when she was done with them. However, Kate would never dream of asking Beth that question.

After Bob finished, Connor looked to Beth for

her input. Beth was there to brief the task force on what she had learned from Jimmy Potts but also because of her expertise on this recent case. Connor had met Beth years ago while working on another case. Beth had been with the Behavioral Science Unit at the FBI, and Connor trusted her spot-on analyses.

"When I talked with Jimmy Potts, he said that Joel had mentioned there was difficultly between the two boys early on. The problems became worse as time passed. Jimmy mentioned that Joel had told his brother, Fletcher, that Logan would do things and make it look like Cole had done them, beginning early in their childhood." Beth stopped and let them process the information.

"Nevertheless, Jimmy said that Joel never mentioned Cole causing any problems or having nightmares. I can only assume he did have triggers when he first moved in but Joel never mentioned them to Fletcher or Jimmy."

"Was Fletcher living with Joel when Cole first moved in?" Bob asked.

"No, Fletcher moved in years later, after his wife passed away," Kate interjected.

"I did, however, call a friend over at the bureau and have him look into Logan's past," Beth said. "He was able to tell me the name of a psychiatrist who had seen Logan as a child and into early adulthood. Logan has had a drug abuse problem from…," Beth referred to her notes. "It looks like from middle school on."

"Was the bureau able to get the name of the psychiatrist?" Kate asked.

"Dr. Griffin Bennett. However, with HIPAA and patient confidentiality, it will be hard, if not impossible, to obtain the records. You'll need to talk to the DA about this. Also, if I may ask you all a favor: The information I'm giving to you, and my source, are to not to leave this room."

Beth looked at the detectives. "My friend was able to see some of the personal information and noted that Logan had set a trashcan on fire at the school."

"So, in short, Logan was acting out to get attention once Cole moved in with the Sawyers?" Connor asked.

"It would appear to me that the real hardcore episodes began to surface around the time when Cole was adopted. I can only assume that Logan felt that the Sawyers wouldn't adopt Cole. Then, when they did, all hell broke loose in Logan's world. Cole was Logan's trigger," Beth finished.

"We don't have enough to get the DA to sign off to talk to Dr. Bennett or pull records yet. Nor do we know for sure whether Logan murdered his father and Fletcher then set the fire," Kate said.

"Unfortunately, you won't be able to talk to Dr. Bennett, I'm afraid. My source tells me he passed away unexpectedly about a year ago," Beth added.

"So, if Cole refuses to go into Dan's on his own, if we go back up into the mountains and encounter him, is there any way we can get him to trust us?" asked Kate.

"I'm afraid that, without seeing his behavior, I really can't say," Beth said, looking at her wristwatch. "Nonetheless, I'll keep digging and see what I can find. I do need to get to my next appointment. If I hear anything more from the bureau, I'll gladly pass it on."

Beth stood and handed her reports to Connor. As Connor walked out Beth, Kate's desk phone rang.

"Logan, thank you for calling us. Kate tells me you have information regarding your father's murder,"

Connor said a few hours later, watching Logan's body language.

"I'm sorry to bother you, detectives," Logan said. "I know you're very busy."

He scratched at a scab on his arm before continuing. "Cole came to my house yesterday evening."

"And?" Connor prompted

"He confessed to me ... that he shot my dad and Mr. Potts, then set fire to the house and left."

Logan watched as the two detectives processed the information.

"He came to your house? Where is he now?" Connor asked.

"Don't know. After he told me what he did, I asked him to stay but he refused. He got up and left. I guess he just needed to get it off his chest."

"Do you have the paper he wrote this confession on? You know, with Cole unable to speak, he would have had to write it down," Kate said.

"Oh, yes."

Logan pulled a folded piece of paper from his pocket and handed it to Kate. Kate immediately noticed the paper wasn't from the notebook they had left Cole in the mountains. One thing was very clear: Logan's attitude today was very different from what it had been the other day, when they had first interviewed him.

"Did Cole bring this confession to you or did he write it in front of you?" Kate asked.

"Oh, he sat there and wrote it in front of me," Logan said.

Kate looked at Connor and passed the paper to him.

"I'm only trying to help," Logan said as he stood up, ready to leave.

"Thank you," Kate said.

Logan walked to the door. As he put his hand on the doorknob, Connor asked, "Can I ask you what he was wearing?"

Turning, Logan thought for a second and said, "Black slacks and a gray shirt."

Connor wrote it down.

"Did he tell you where he's staying, by any chance?" Connor asked.

"No. I assume with a friend from that nerd school."

"Thank you," Connor said.

Connor and Kate went back to their office. Connor looked over the list of things they had left with Cole. When they had seen Cole, he was wearing a pair of faded blue jeans and a tee-shirt. Nether Kate nor Connor had purchased black slacks or a gray shirt.

"Do we have a sample of Cole's handwriting?" Connor asked.

"Connor, you can't for a minute think, of all the people in the world, that Cole committed such a heinous crime and that he would go to Logan and confess, do you?"

"No, but legally we have to prove that this is wrong. Kate, I know you want Cole to be innocent of any wrongdoing. I think you're correct, but he does have a troubled past. I just don't want you to be upset or hurt if, for any reason, he's guilty."

Kate sat silent for a few minutes.

"I wonder if I applied for guardianship of Cole, when all this is over, if the court would allow him to stay with me. If he wanted that," Kate said.

"Kate, I think that at age eighteen, he doesn't really need a guardianship. Maybe a home to live in while he's still in school."

Kate turned her attention back to the reports on her desk.

CHAPTER 13

Professor Luca DeAngelo held a copy of Cole's confession and studied it carefully. Walking over to his desk, he sat in an old brown leather chair, which Connor could see had a lot of mileage on it—probably from long before its use on this campus.

The professor looked to be in his early fifties. He had salt-and-pepper hair and a beard of the same hue. He was dressed in khaki pants and a blue button-down shirt and wore thick glasses with black frames. His frame was thin and he had narrow shoulders. He was a thinking man who worked with his mind, not his hands. Connor guessed the glasses were probably the result of too many hours spent solving mathematical problems or creating them for his higher-level students, like Cole.

The professor continued to study the document in his hands, carefully re-reading it. He traced the letters with his left index finger.

"Professor DeAngelo, thank you for looking this over. I assumed that if anyone had a sample of Cole's handwriting, it would be you," Connor said.

As the professor retrieved two documents from his file cabinet and began comparing them to Connor's paper, Connor looked up at the math equations on the blackboard. He had no clue how to solve them or why anyone would want to. The blackboard was a maze of numbers, letters, and symbols in white chalk that looked like a work of abstract art. A chalk outline of a three-dimensional box was labeled with numbers and letters: $2x$ on the front side, $K+M+J+I$ on the bottom front of the box, $2x$ on the side, and $6x$ on top. Connor's eyes were riveted to the mysterious equations. Why on earth would anyone need to know the answers?

"Detective," Professor DeAngelo said, pausing a few seconds before repeating, "Detective," to get Connor's attention.

"Oh, I was just looking." Connor pointed to the blackboard. "It almost looks like a work of art."

"Ah, yes." DeAngelo smiled at Connor's comment. "Math is, I guess, art in numbers."

He cleared his throat and returned his focus to the three papers in front of him. After a pause, he spoke up again.

"I'm no expert on handwriting, you understand. However, in looking at Cole's handwriting here and on this other report he turned in, I see that the Ts are quite different. Note that the slope isn't the same, nor are the Is. Beyond that, if you look at the overall spacing of the lettering and slope of the handwriting, I would have to say this is not the handwriting of Cole Sawyer." The professor put the three papers on his desk and turned them for Connor to look at.

Connor could clearly see what the professor was saying.

"Furthermore," DeAngelo said, "I have to tell you, I've known Cole and his father, Joel, for several years. I can't imagine Cole doing such a thing as this." The professor pointed to the confession.

"Is there any way I could take these papers, for samples of Cole's handwriting? The fire destroyed everything and we have nothing to compare it to other than these."

"Detective, under normal circumstances, I would say no, as this is the student's property."

"We could get the DA to…" Connor started but was interrupted.

"I fully understand that the law can force me to hand over these documents. But I would much rather give you a copy. If you'll wait here, I'll make copies for you." The professor got up and left the classroom without another word. Several minutes later, he returned, put Cole's papers in the file cabinet, and pushed two copies across the desk toward Connor.

"I must leave for a time. What you do with these when I'm gone is up to you, Detective Maxwell. But before I go, I want to tell you that Cole is a very gifted young man. The United States government has already looked into hiring him as soon as he graduates. The boy has a brilliant mind. I can tell you, never in my life have I seen such a magnificent student. I want your word that if this should need to go to court, you will go through the legal channels to request these papers. Do we have an understanding?"

Connor felt like he was back in school. He simply nodded his acceptance. With that, Professor

DeAngelo turned and left the classroom. Connor picked up the copies and left as well.

---

Kate waited patiently at Dan's Coffee Shop to talk with Logan's ex-girlfriend, Abigail Harper. She arrived a few minutes after three o'clock, ordered a latte, and asked for Kate. The barista pointed to Kate's table. Kate stood as Abigail—a petite, professionally dressed blonde in her twenties—approached.

"You must be Abigail? Kate said, shaking her hand. "Thank you for agreeing to speak with me."

"Detective, I'm not sure how I can help you, but Logan's father was a very nice man. I can't imagine anyone wanting to hurt Joel. Logan, not so much."

"How long did you and Logan date?" Kate asked.

Abigail was still getting settled at the table. Once she hung her purse over the chair back, she turned to Kate and sighed heavily.

"We dated for about a year," Abigail said, taking a sip from her cup as if she could drown out the memory of herself and Logan.

"If I may ask, why did you two break up?"

Abigail smiled at the question. "Logan has a drug problem. I assume you already know that. Mr. Sawyer had him in several drug programs, but nothing worked. I told Logan he had to want to quit, for himself. He told me he didn't think he had a problem." Abigail looked down at the table in thought.

"Abigail, if not for the drugs, would you have stayed with Logan?"

"No, he was a bully. He picked on Cole all the time. Joel would get him a job but he'd last only a few days before he'd pick a fight with another employee or the boss and be fired. Logan thinks he's superior to everyone. He dislikes people of color and hates people who don't think like he does." Abigail shrugged as if unable to understand Logan's actions.

"You mentioned he picked on Cole. We have reason to believe that Logan would do things and then try to make it look like Cole did them, to get Cole in trouble. Do you know if that was true?"

"Logan despised Cole. He would go out of his way to make trouble for Cole. He didn't like that Cole was a part of his family and he really wanted nothing more than to rid the family of Cole. He hated that Cole excelled in school and that his father was so proud of Cole. Logan was a very jealous person when it came to Cole but there was no reason he should have been. Joel did just as much for Logan. He bought him a fancy car and set him up in a nice house, paid his credit card bills, got him jobs, you name it. Nothing mattered to Logan except getting Cole out of his way. He called him a mutt ... a stray."

"When was the last time you saw or talked to Logan?"

"I work as a legal assistant to Mr. Sawyer's attorney. Joel came in to make some changes in his will."

Kate interrupted. "No, I meant when was the last time you saw or spoke to Logan?"

"Oh, I see. Shortly after Joel made the changes to his will, Logan came into our law office, furious. He demanded to speak to the attorney. Luckily, Attorney Shelton was out of the office. I tried to explain that his father had the right to change his will if he wanted to. Logan pushed me aside and ran to Attorney Shelton's office door, which was locked. He came back and tossed everything off my desk, pushed me onto the floor, and then left."

"Did you call the police?"

"No, but I called Mr. Sawyer. More as a friend than as a legal assistant. I told him Logan was very upset. I was worried about Joel and what Logan would do to him. Mr. Sawyer said that Logan must have gone to the house when he, Fletcher, and Cole were gone and seen the new will before Mr. Sawyer put his copy into his safety deposit box."

"Abigail, I assume that, due to client confidentiality, you can't tell me what was in the will that upset Logan," said Kate.

"That's correct, but if you can get the DA to sign off, I know Attorney Shelton would be happy to give you a copy of the will."

Kate sighed. They still didn't have enough evidence for the DA to sign off on anything.

"Detective Stroup, I understand all too well what a pain in the ass the DA can be with things like this, but I need my job and…"

"I understand," Kate said.

"While I can't give you the contents and details of the will, do you know Joel's roommate's brother, Jimmy Potts?"

"Yes, I do. Why do you ask?"

"Simple. Fletcher was told to give a copy of the will to his brother, Jimmy," Abigail said.

# CHAPTER 14

Connor, Kate, and Sundae arrived at their appointment with Cole's caseworker. This time, they had to find a way to talk Cole down from the mountain. Connor and Kate were increasingly worried about Cole surviving in the bitter cold, to say nothing of the visit to the campsite by the black bear. Thankfully, Cole had known to bang together two pots and the old bear had wandered off.

Maggie Ortega was a short woman, only about five feet tall, with a slim build and hair that favored the orange—rather than red—side of the spectrum.

"Hi," she said as she shook hands with each detective before bending down to Sundae. "You must be Sundae, the law enforcement puppy I've read so much about in the papers."

"Thank you so much for meeting with us, Ms. Ortega," Connor said.

"Please, call me Maggie. Why don't we go into my office to chat?"

The detectives followed her down a drab hallway to a small office. She motioned for them to take a seat on a small couch, then pulled up a chair for herself.

"I keep hearing all the TV reports and, frankly, they worry me," Maggie said, clasping her hands together in her lap.

"Maggie, what the TV reports aren't saying, and we don't want this information leaked, is where Cole is. That's why we thought you may be of help," Kate said, tucking a strand of auburn hair behind one ear.

"Where might that be?" Maggie asked, a confused look on her face.

"He has been spotted at Dan's Coffee and Pasty shop, looking for food in their trash bin. The owner called us, so we went out the next day and waited at around the same time," Connor said.

"My God," Maggie gasped, one hand flying to her mouth.

"He refused the plate of food from us the following day. We called out to him but he bolted across the road and into the mountains," Connor added.

"My word." Maggie reached her hands to her mouth again.

Kate sighed heavily. "Maggie, to say that Cole had a troubled childhood is an understatement—at least until he moved in with the Sawyers. We know that from his records. Connor and I tried to follow him but we lost him. We went back later and found an area where he may have made a makeshift campsite. We took blankets, a tent, food, a cookstove, clothes, a coat, and gloves, but we need to get him into a safe place off that mountain. Is there anything you can tell us that could help us make him understand that we don't want to hurt him?"

Maggie looked beyond them and out her office window, lost in thought.

"Maggie," Connor prompted.

"As with any organization like ours, a boy in our care has privacy. Now, given the circumstances and his well-being, may I ask, as you both have, to keep this information confidential?" Maggie looked to both detectives.

"Yes," Connor said.

"You have our word," Kate said.

"I've known Cole from the time he came into

the program as a baby. He was left at a fire station as an infant. I was with the state at that time. He was placed in several foster homes but things never seemed to work out. As he got older, the harder it became. The couple who fostered him as an infant was able to take him only until the age of eighteen months. Then it was on to the next foster home. As he got older, parents wanting him became few and far between.

"Often, parents looking to adopt come into the program with certain expectations of the child. Cole was never a good match. I had to remove him from several foster homes because the parents were more interested in collecting the money rather than taking care of the child. Once he was abused to the point that he couldn't talk, I brought him here to the boys' home," Maggie said as a tear ran down her cheek.

"The foster care system is by far not a perfect one. It works for some, while for others it doesn't. Just like some foster families are kind and loving, while others are in it more for the money."

Maggie stood, turned, and walked behind her desk. There, she bent down to a small filing cabinet and retrieved a small silver key from a purple lanyard around her neck. Maggie unlocked the cabinet and pulled out a stack of what looked like letters tied with a ribbon. As she sat down, she looked at the stack with sadness.

"These were all written by Cole to his mother and father throughout the time I knew him," Maggie said, holding tightly to the letters before handing them to Kate.

"But I thought he never knew his mother or father," Connor said.

"That's correct, but Cole never gave up hope that someday they'd come looking him. He asked me to keep the letters for him. After the Sawyers decided to adopt Cole, I asked him if he wanted the letters. He said no but I could never bring myself to get rid of them."

"Did you read them?" Kate asked.

Maggie sighed and shook her head no.

"Were the Sawyers and Cole a good match?" Connor asked.

"Yes and no. Their older son began acting out. He had been an only child. When Cole moved in, and especially once he was adopted, the older son seemed to be filled with hate. Cole was so happy someone understood how much his grades and education meant to him. You do know that Cole is gifted in math?" Maggie asked.

"Yes," Connor said. "In fact, I talked to one of

his professors yesterday. He said he'd never in all his years come across a student as gifted as Cole."

Maggie smiled.

"Was Cole the first foster child the Sawyers took in or had they fostered others?" Kate asked.

"I knew Joel from a reading club I belong to and happened to mention Cole to him one day, never thinking twice about it. At the next meeting, Joel asked about Cole. He'd purchased several math puzzle books for him and asked me to give them to Cole. For every puzzle book he completed, Cole wrote Joel a thank-you letter. He asked me to give the letters to Joel. When I did, Joel said, "Well, I need to find some more for the boy." The math puzzle books went back and forth for several months until one day Joel said he and his wife wanted to meet Cole.

"I agreed. We all met for dinner at Lakota Restaurant. Cole was so excited to meet Mr. and Mrs. Sawyer. They met and didn't mention their intentions to me that night. The next day, I found a message on my answering machine from Joel, stating that they would be happy to take Cole into their home and asking what they needed to do. After they filled out their paperwork, I told them both at our first meeting that Cole had previously been placed in several homes. They told me they were not worried about that. Once the Sawyers went through the process and were approved, Cole moved in."

"Did they mention any stressors with Cole?" Connor asked.

"At first, Cole had some bedwetting issues in the new environment but seemed to grow out of them. Mrs. Sawyer told me that the first time he wet the bed, she found him in their basement, naked. I assumed Cole thought that if he wet the bed, he would be punished. Mrs. Sawyer brought him upstairs, had him bathe and dress, and told him they'd get through this with him. From what I understand, the issue happened a few more times but Cole never wet the bed after that."

"Maggie, what can we do to get Cole to come down from the mountain and trust us?" Kate asked.

Maggie pondered the question. "I'd be willing to go up there with you both. He knows me, so maybe…"

"We could give it a try," Kate said, looking at Connor.

"I don't think we'd get too much pushback on that," Connor replied.

"How about tomorrow morning? But you have to wear warm clothes and boots."

Maggie agreed. Connor and Kate stood. Just as Kate reached the door, she turned to Maggie.

"When Cole comes back, he's going to need a place to stay…"

"He can always come back here," Maggie said.

"If he'd stay with me, I'd be happy to take him in," Kate said.

CHAPTER 15

Jimmy Potts pushed his wheelchair over to the end table and motioned for the detectives to sit down. Detectives Barton and Harris sat in the small living room.

"May I get either of you something to drink?"

Before they could speak, Jimmy added, "I have water, coffee, or tea."

"No, thank you," Bob answered for both of them.

"Were you able to find Mr. Sawyer's latest will by any chance?" Detective Harris asked.

Jimmy reached into the side pouch of his wheelchair and fished his hand around. He pulled out the will, which he handed to Detective Barton. Bob carefully removed the will from the outer sleeve and unfolded it.

"We understand from a source that Logan Sawyer became upset with Joel's latest will," Grant said as Bob read the document.

"My brother, Fletcher, had mentioned that. He told me that's why Joel insisted he keep his copy over here with me...In case he needed it if Joel passed first."

Bob continued reading the will line for line until he got to the second page.

"Maybe this is why," Bob said. It says, 'In the event that I should pass away first, I leave my home at 2255 Decker Avenue, free and clear, to my best friend, Fletcher Potts. I also request that he allow my son, Cole Sawyer, to live there as long as he wishes. After the passing of my friend, Fletcher Potts, the home will pass on to my son, Cole Sawyer."

"Yes. Fletcher originally mentioned that all assets were to be equally divided between the two boys. After Fletcher had lived with Joel for about... let me see," Jimmy thought for a moment. "I think it was about two years, Joel felt it would be too hard on Fletcher to be uprooted from the home if something happened to Joel. He also knew that Fletcher would look out for Cole. Joel told Fletcher he would never trust Logan to look after Cole and his well-being. From what I understand, Cole's education was all paid for by Joel. But he felt that Fletcher would allow Cole to live there should something happen. And as I said, he told Fletcher he couldn't trust Logan where Cole was concerned," Jimmy said, looking at both detectives.

Bob glanced at the document again. "The notary stamp's date is about a month before Joel and Fletcher were killed," he said. "That would certainly give Logan a motive," he added under his breath.

"What did you say? I'm sorry, I didn't hear you," Jimmy said, turning up his hearing aid.

"Nothing, nothing at all. Just thinking out loud. Mr. Potts, would you mind if I took the will?" Bob asked. "I'll make a copy and return the original to you."

"No, I don't think Fletcher will need it now."

Connor walked into the house and glanced around. He found Carlos in his room, busy with homework at his new desk. The sitter looked up, her earbuds in place. She quickly grabbed her coat and books.

"See you tomorrow," the babysitter said, and was out the front door.

Connor walked into Carlos' room and put his hand on his shoulder.

"Hi, buddy. Working on your homework?"

"I wanted to get it done so we could go visit Nana tonight, if that's okay."

"Sure. We can grab a bite to eat and drop by the hospital. Let me know when you're ready to go."

Connor's phone chimed. He saw a text to him and Kate.

"Got Joel's will. I can see a possible motive for both Joel and Fletcher being murdered. I can only assume that Cole was to be in that fire as well. I'll bring the will in tomorrow morning."

---

Kate set the fast-food bag with the fries and burger on her kitchen table. She read the text from Bob, then opened the bag. The aroma from the burger and fries made her mouth water. She read Bob's text and saw that she had missed a call on her home phone. She was about to delete it, as the only person who ever left a voicemail on her landline was her ex asking to borrow money. She took a large bite of the burger and hit play on the old machine.

"Hi, Kate, this is Maggie, Maggie Ortega. We talked today…I was wondering if you are serious about taking in Cole? I talked to my supervisor and he feels that even though Cole is eighteen, he would be much better off in a good home…"

With that, the old answering machine disconnected the call mid-sentence. Kate took another bite from the burger, ran two French fries through the pool of ketchup, and wondered what was in the will that could make a son want to kill his father. She recalled her meeting with Abigail, Logan's ex-girlfriend, and her statement about Logan and his drug habit. But from the way she made it sound, Joel had given money to Logan. Kate felt sure that Joel did so not knowing he was handing Logan money to support his drug habit. Still, what could Logan's motive be?

She had just taken another bite of her burger when the doorbell rang. Grabbing a few French fries, she went to the door and opened it.

"What do you want?" Kate said, eating her fries and staring at her ex-husband, Jackson.

Jackson Rizzo was a handsome, six-foot-tall, muscular man with blonde hair and blue eyes that had captivated Kate the first time she had looked into them. His friends called him "Ace" due to his love of playing cards and winning. Ace was a smooth talker both in and out of the bedroom.

"I was just driving by and thought…"

Kate interrupted, "What? 'I haven't made Kate's life miserable in a while so I thought I'd drop by?'" She gave him a disdainful look.

"Kate, I miss you."

Ace used his index finger to wipe a dab of ketchup from the corner of her mouth, then put it in his own. "Tastes good. Got more?"

He pushed by her and went into the kitchen, where he grabbed a handful of fries.

Kate shut the front door. "And here I thought I took the trash out last night," she said, spinning on her heels and returning to the kitchen just as Ace took another fry from the bag and stuffed it into his mouth.

"Kate, we really need to talk."

"We have nothing to talk about. What is it? A school night for your girlfriend and she can't come out to play?" Kate asked, taking another bite from her burger.

Ace moved closer to Kate and rested his forearms on her shoulders.

"I still love you and I know you still love me," he said, looking into her eyes.

Kate looked at him. Yes, she had loved him a long time ago. They had plans like any other couple but Ace hated that she worked for the police department. Soon, he found other interests besides Kate. The first girlfriend was a few years younger than Kate. The next one was even younger. In fact, at first Kate had thought she was still in high school. It was this lollipop, as Kate referred to her, whom Kate had caught with Ace in their bed after a long shift at work. After that, the only thing left between them was the divorce.

Ace continued to see his little lollipop. For the first few months after the divorce, Kate seemed to run into the two of them everywhere she went.

Returning to the present moment, Kate removed his arms from her shoulders, turned him toward the front door, and pushed him.

"Ace, there's the door you walked out of. Why don't you do an encore one last time?"

Kate stood her ground and watched Ace walk out the door. She sat down as memories of the two of them tumbled through her mind.

Kate exited the elevator and saw Connor already at his desk, talking on the phone. Sundae was curled up in the bed next to Connor's desk. Kate walked over and the little beagle raised her head. Kate petted Sundae, stroking the dog's soft ears before walking around to her desk and removing her coat. She noticed a stack of papers on her desk and saw the first page contained the words "Last Will and Testament of Joel Sawyer."

Kate read the first page as she listened to the one-sided conversation between Connor and whomever he was talking to, whom she assumed could be a realtor.

"So, in looking at the website, you can see the house at 2255 Decker Avenue before the fire? I realize the house is no longer there, but can you give me an idea of what this house was worth before the fire?" Connor asked. He looked over at Kate and motioned for her to turn the first page of the will.

Kate did so and saw the new verbiage, stating that the house would no longer be sold, with the proceeds divided between the two sons, Logan and Cole. Instead, the house would be left free and clear to Fletcher, with Cole allowed to live there. Another stipulation stated that the house would go to Cole upon Fletcher's death.

Connor thanked the realtor and hung up the phone.

Kate held up the second page of the will, looking at Connor.

"You think this was Logan's motive, the house?" Kate asked.

"The realtor is going to run comps for the area and email them to me as soon as she has them. When she looked at the neighborhood, she said that houses in that area are worth a lot depending on square footage and the amount of land. She told me they can get a pretty accurate figure. Also, if we can talk to Joel's insurance agent, we can find out how much the house was insured for."

Kate stood up from her desk. "We need to get going. We're supposed to meet Maggie at Dan's in an hour."

---

At the head of the trail, Connor and Sundae led the way up the mountain. Kate felt a chill as she remembered the day when she and Connor had come back in the snowstorm. In contrast, today was sunny but the temperature was in the forties. Connor's backpack was filled with new supplies for

Cole, in case their quest to bring him back down the mountain was unsuccessful.

"Cole, this is Maggie. I need to talk to you," Maggie called out every few minutes, hoping that Cole would hear and recognize her voice, if not her name.

After about an hour on the trail, Connor heard the sound of snow crunching in the distance. He stopped and closed his eyes to heighten his sense of hearing. When he opened his eyes, he turned and pointed to the right. He motioned to Maggie to take the lead.

"Cole, please, we need to talk," Maggie called out as she walked around Connor and Sundae. Connor quietly followed Maggie at a distance to keep her in his sight in case it was a bear they'd heard and not Cole.

As Connor watched, Maggie held Cole, hugging him. Connor and Kate held back and sat on a downed log while Maggie talked to Cole. Maggie had managed to get closer to Cole than anyone had since the fire. Would she be able to convince him to come back with them?

CHAPTER 16

As Maggie emerged from the trees, Kate felt a sense of relief. However, the feeling was short-lived, as she saw that Maggie was alone. Connor noted the concerned look on Kate's face.

"Well?" Kate called out to Maggie.

"He wants to get a few things and bring them back. He didn't know that Joel and Fletcher perished in the fire." Maggie held out a piece of paper that Cole had written on.

"I can help him break down the camp," Connor said, standing up.

Maggie shook her head no.

"He needs some time to digest this new information. He's really torn up inside, hearing about Joel and Fletcher," Maggie said, dabbing at tears as they rolled down her cheek.

Connor took the paper on which Cole had written his responses to Maggie and read it.

"You asked him if he knew what happened to Joel and Fletcher?" Connor glanced down at the paper and continued to read out loud. "He said they were hurt and bleeding on the floor when he came out of his bedroom."

Connor turned the paper over. "He didn't mention if he saw anyone in the house before or after he found them?" he asked Maggie, looking for more answers on the paper in his hand.

"No, I didn't ask that question, Detective. He was very distressed once he learned Joel was dead. He cried. I didn't get much out of him after that. I felt it was more important to explain who you and Kate are and that you're only trying to get him to a safer place," Maggie explained.

Connor folded the paper and tucked it in his pocket as Maggie sat down to wait with them. The sound of footsteps tromping through the snow became louder. Then Cole emerged from the trees, carrying his clothes, blankets, and notebook. Maggie stood and took Cole gently by the arm.

"Cole, this is Kate Stroup, Connor Maxwell,

and their dog, Sundae." Cole took a tentative step forward, looking them over with caution. "They only want to help you," Maggie added.

Cole stared at the badge clipped to Connor's belt. Maggie noticed.

"Kate, Connor, and Sundae are with the Lakewood Police Department. They want to find the person who hurt your father and his friend."

Cole's eyes went from Maggie to Connor to Kate. Sundae walked over to Cole. He bent to pet her, then smiled for the first time.

"Cole, do you want me to get anything else from the camp?" Connor asked, slowly and a little louder than normal.

Cole shook his head no.

Maggie whispered in Connor's ear. "You can talk in a normal tone. Cole can hear you just fine. You can talk to him like you'd speak to anyone else."

"Let's get off this mountain. I can come back here and bring the rest of the things down later," Connor said.

Maggie reached over to Cole as they came closer.

The four walked down the mountainside with Sundae leading the way, following their trail back with her white-tipped tail high in the air.

"Cole, Kate said you can stay at her house if you'd like," Maggie said.

Cole quickly wrote in his notebook. "Can't I go back home?"

"Cole, the house burnt down to the ground. There's nothing left for you to go back to, sweetie," Maggie said.

Cole stopped and furrowed his dark brown eyebrows together as if unable to comprehend that the home he had lived in was completely gone.

"There's nothing left to stay in," Kate said.

"Can I go see?" Cole wrote and showed Kate.

"Why don't we get a hot meal first?" Kate suggested.

Cole motioned to his pockets and Kate instinctively understood.

"Cole, we'll pay. Don't worry."

---

At Dan's, Cole went into the men's room and cleaned up as best he could, splashing soap and water on his face and arms. After they had eaten a hot meal, Connor drove them all over to the lot at 2255 Decker Avenue. Maggie followed in her car. Cole walked around the charred wood that was left behind. He went over to where he had last seen Joel and Fletcher and began to cry. Maggie reached over and hugged him.

---

Maggie sat beside Cole while Connor and Kate sat on the other side of the table in the box at the Lakewood Police Department. While the audio captured only Connor and Kate's questions, the video recorded body language. One camera focused on Cole, the other on the paper on which Cole wrote, so they could refer back to it later if necessary.

Beth Ellis stood outside the room and listened on the other side of the one-way glass. While she couldn't read what he was writing, she studied Cole's movements and facial expressions. From her perspective, it was like watching a silent movie. Beth made a note on her pad about how serious the boy looked. He didn't seem to be trying to hide anything from the detectives. Rather, he had the look of a much older person faced with an irreplaceable loss. Sad, Beth thought, to have had such an awful start in life, with no parents who wanted you, followed by a string of bad foster homes, then losing the one family that loved you.

"Cole, you wrote that you heard and smelled something as you came out of your bedroom. Do you remember hearing a gunshot?" Connor asked.

"I was listening to my iPod and doing my homework. I smelled gasoline and smoke. I thought I heard a muffled pop when I opened my bedroom door. The hallway was filled with thick smoke. I ran into the living room and found my dad and Fletcher on the floor by the fireplace. At first, I thought the fire had started from the fireplace but the smell of gasoline was in the air. The kitchen was on fire as well as the curtains, the den, my dad's study, everything. I tried to reach them. That was when my pant leg caught fire."

Cole stopped writing. His hand was shaking so badly, he had to put the pen down on the table.

"Cole, take your time," Kate said softly. "I know how hard it is to relive this but it's important that we find out how this happened to your father."

Cole quickly grabbed the pen and wrote. "He wasn't my father." He looked at everyone and continued to write. "Joel was my dad. Anyone can be a father but it takes a good man to be a dad."

"You are so right about that," Connor said.

"Cole, do you remember hearing or seeing

anyone in the house besides your dad and Fletcher?" Kate asked.

Cole wrote "no," and underlined it.

"At what point did you leave the house?" Connor asked.

"The flames were surrounding me. I tried to reach my dad and Fletcher but it was so hot. The fire was all around me on the carpet. I panicked and ran back to my bedroom, opened my window, and jumped out." As he finished writing, he began rubbing the burn marks on his left arm from his childhood.

"Where did you go when you left the house?" Connor asked.

"The forest behind our house," Cole wrote. "I never looked back. I was scared."

"You didn't think to run to the other houses on the street for help?" Connor asked.

"No, I'm afraid of people," Cole wrote. He continued to rub the burn scars.

Connor sat for a moment without saying anything.

"Did you see anyone outside the house when you jumped out the window?" Kate asked.

Cole thought before answering, "No."

"Do you remember hearing anything outside?" Kate asked.

"Yes. Rap music, loud rap music," Cole wrote.

"Do you remember what the song was?" Kate asked.

"I've heard it before, but I don't know the title," he wrote.

"Where do you remember hearing it?" Kate asked.

Cole wrote, "Once Dad asked Logan to pick me up at school. Logan had it playing on a CD in his car. Logan plays his music really loud."

CHAPTER 17

Cole's living arrangements were decided before they left the PD. Having known Maggie for years, he wanted to stay at Maggie's house, at least for the next few days. However, first Connor and Kate took Cole shopping for some new clothes and essentials that he would need for day-to-day living. Connor also took the opportunity to study Cole's behavior while they were out. He noted that Cole had simple taste, unlike Logan's designer jeans and shirts and expensive car. Cole was a down-to-earth kid except for his gift for math. When Kate showed Cole a pair of slacks, he and Connor both shook their heads no. Cole wrote, "Just jeans, please." Then he smiled at Connor.

"Both of you are a pair!" Kate said, putting the slacks back on the rack.

The one thing that seemed to light up Cole's eyes was a hoodie with the Red Sox team logo. While the team hoodies were more expensive than the other hoodies, Connor had him try one on for size. Then Connor put it into the basket to purchase it. When he did that, Cole smiled and wrote "Thank you."

They dropped off Cole, with several bags in tow, at Maggie's. He hugged Kate and Connor and thanked them again. Then they headed directly back to the police department for a meeting with Beth, Barton, and Harris.

"It's easy to see why Joel and his wife took to Cole. He's a good kid," Connor said to Kate.

---

Everyone was waiting as Kate and Connor stepped off the elevator.

"There they are, the parents of the year! Why don't you two just get married and have a few of your own? You know Sundae needs a mommy and daddy," Bob called out, half-joking and half-serious. Grant and Beth joined in on the banter, making

Connor blush. It seemed that everyone in the department knew there was something between the two of them except for Connor and Kate, who kept pushing those feelings to the side.

"Okay, okay! Let's get to work, you bunch of cupids. Valentine's Day is in February," Connor said.

On the way to the conference room, Connor went to his desk, with Sundae scampering behind him. He got Sundae's bowl from his drawer and filled it with bottled water, then continued to the conference room.

"Where are our water bowls?" Grant asked.

Connor turned, left the room, and returned with five water bottles, which he set on the table.

"If any of you want kibble, you'll need to ask Sundae," Connor said, taking his seat.

After the chuckling stopped, Kate got up and handed several sheets of paper to Bob and Grant.

"Beth, do you still have yours?" Kate asked.

Beth nodded that she did.

"We have the video feed of Cole's interview. As you already know, Cole had to write his responses. The purpose of the video today is to look at body language and get Beth's input. She was present during our interview," Kate said.

Connor dimmed the lights and started the video. He handed Beth the remote so that she could stop the video any time she wanted to interject her thoughts. Beth stood beside the whiteboard. The screen showed a freeze-frame of the interview between Kate, Connor, Maggie, and Cole.

"First, I'd like you to note Cole's posture and watch his hands throughout. He's visibly upset over losing his father. That is very clear. He also underlines things that he feels strongly about. Check page two. You'll see the word 'no' underlined. I sent this off to a handwriting agent whom I worked with at the bureau. Let's look at the video. Then I'll go into what the agent told me."

Beth resumed the video. The detectives watched and referred to Cole's written responses. Bob used a yellow highlighter to note certain answers.

Beth froze a frame on the video where Cole had set the pen down on the table. "Note how his hands shake as he recounts how he tried to save his dad and his pant leg caught on fire. You can clearly see that this is a trigger for him. He sets the pen down, then rubs the burn scars on his forearms. First, on the left arm and then on the right. Now compare this to the other questions that either Kate or

Connor ask him," Beth said. She restarted the video.

After it ended, Connor turned the lights back on.

"As I stated before, I sent Cole's responses to an agent I worked with at the bureau. He called me this morning. He believes that Cole's written responses were honest and straightforward. When you asked the question about his father, he corrected both detectives, stating that Joel was his dad, not just his father. The underlining of certain words that were dark in ink, as well as written with more pressure on the paper, showed that this young man truly cared about his dad. The agent didn't see the video, so he couldn't see Cole's hand shaking. However, under a microscope, he detected a pen shake, even after the trigger. I told him this morning about Cole's past. He stated that would be consistent with the triggers of burns and fire. Now, with that said, can we take this into a courtroom? Yes and no. By that, I mean this alone will do nothing if the DA decides to pin this on Cole." Beth returned to her seat.

Connor drove the unmarked car through an upscale neighborhood. Money was spelled on the address of every house on the tree-lined street. Each home's landscape was meticulously maintained. Any of the residences could have been on the cover of Architectural Digest. Fitting that Logan would reside in a posh home. Joel seemed to want the very best for both of his children, biological or adopted. Kate thought to herself that if Joel had come into Cole's life sooner, maybe Cole would still be able to talk.

A taxi pulled over to the curb in front of Logan's home. From the house teetered a scantily clad woman wearing stiletto heels and carrying a purse. She got into the cab. Connor squinted and looked again to be sure.

"Isn't that China who works over on Central?" he asked as he started to follow the cab.

"Sure looks like her," Kate answered. "So, Logan has a taste for the ladies of the evening, too. This young man better hope he never runs out of Daddy's money."

Connor waited until the cab stopped in front of a sleazy motel, known by the cops as a no-tell motel. He drove up as China got out of the car and the cab driver pulled away. China noticed Connor and Kate as they walked toward her. She ran her hand from Connor's neck down to his muscular chest.

"Hi there, sweetie. Long time no see. Who's your girlfriend?"

"This is Detective Kate Stroup. China, we need to talk," Connor said.

"Honey, I ain't done nothing."

"We just want to talk, okay?"

China turned and plopped herself on top of the unmarked car. She crossed her legs seductively, smiled, and licked her lips.

"Shoot, big guy."

"How do you know Logan Sawyer?" Connor asked.

"Who?" China looked confused.

"The John's house you just left. And, by the way, I didn't know you made house calls these days," Connor said.

"Oh, sweetie, a workin' girl has to do what she has to do, and he paid well," China said.

"So, you were on the job at that house?"

"Are you going to arrest me?"

"If you cooperate, we can forget this little matter," Connor said.

"That would all depend on what you want,

sweetie," China said, running the tip of her shoe along the inside of his leg.

Connor quickly stepped back.

"The guy you just left, what's his name?"

"He said it was Cole. He picked me up over on Central early this morning."

Kate was busily recording the conversation in her notebook.

"I thought you and the girls use the motels," Connor said.

"Honey, this dude paid me extra to go home with him, crazy nut job. Like, batshit crazy. He was so high on drugs and drunk. And what he wanted, well, I can't go into that. You know, privacy issues."

"Funny, I wasn't aware ladies such as yourself had to adhere to HIPAA regulations. "

"More like client confidentiality," said China, giving Connor a sexy smile. "After I was done, he kept rambling about how he hated his brother and his father."

"Did he tell you anything else?"

"Only that his dad tried to write him out of the will," China said.

"Anything else?" Connor asked.

The crackle of the dispatcher over the police

radio could be heard. Kate jumped into the car and took the call.

"Connor, we need to go!" she yelled.

"Thank you, China," Connor said as he slipped her a twenty-dollar bill. She pulled down her blouse and tucked the twenty inside her bra.

"Where are we going?" Connor asked Kate.

"Somehow, the DA got a copy of that bogus confession from Cole. They're arresting him."

CHAPTER 18

Connor started up the car, threw it in drive, and headed toward Maggie's house.

"Have they picked him up yet?" Connor asked Kate.

"I don't know. Sandy only said the DA asked if we still had him. She said she told them no and gave them Maggie's address."

"Shit!" Connor said, slamming his fists on the steering wheel. "Everything we did to build Cole's trust is now out the window. Who the hell gave them a copy of that bogus letter?"

"Three guesses, and the first two don't count," Kate said.

"Logan," Connor said, disgusted, as Kate nodded.

Connor weaved in and out of traffic.

"Call Sandy. Ask who the DA sent over there to arrest him. Maybe we can radio them before they get there. Call Maggie and tell her to stall until we can get there. After that, call the ADA and put her on speakerphone for me." Connor barked the orders as he turned his head from left to right through intersections, driving as fast as he could.

Kate tried to dial as the police unit swerved back and forth, then gave up and asked her cellphone to dial Sandy Curtis.

"Sandy told me they sent over the state police and I'm getting no answer on Maggie's cell or home phone. Do you still want me to call the ADA?" Kate asked.

Connor turned the corner onto Maggie's street, where they could see Maggie in the driveway and Cole already sitting in the back seat of the patrol car. As the state police car pulled away from the curb, Cole looked out the back window with a frightened expression. Connor jumped out of his car and tried to run after the vehicle, but managed to only bang on it.

"Shit!" Connor yelled as he turned back, visibly shaken.

He walked over to Kate and Maggie. Kate was holding Maggie as she cried.

"I trusted you both. You told me you wanted to help Cole, not arrest him! Do you have any idea what being locked in a jail cell will do to this kid? Do you?" Maggie yelled at them.

"Maggie, we think Logan managed to get a bogus confession letter to the DA. Logan will do anything to get Cole out of the picture where his father's estate and money are concerned. The state police will lock him up in our cells and we can request bond. We'll have him put in a cell by himself until we get this all ironed out. I'll call the ADA on my way over to the police department. If you want to follow us there, I can talk the ADA into releasing him, as he isn't a flight risk. We'll do anything we can," Connor said.

Still upset, Maggie said nothing as she spun on her heels and ran into the house. Kate and Connor heard the lock click behind her. Then the garage door opened and Maggie quickly backed out her car. Connor and Kate jumped back into their vehicle and drove to the police department.

"Kate, call Bob and Grant. Request that they put a 24-hour tail on Logan. Tell them what just went down. I'll call the ADA once we get to the PD."

---

There was a media circus outside the police department. Two channels had set up their vans and trucks. Reporters were ready to announce the breaking news. Connor thought someone, probably Logan, had leaked the story to the press in an effort to get the DA's office to do something. He drove toward the back end of the department and motioned Maggie to do the same.

---

Sandy looked up, phone to her ear, as she saw Connor enter. She waved him toward her office.

"It's the ADA. She wants to speak to you," Sandy said, handing the phone to Connor.

"What the hell are you clowns doing? You have the wrong person," Connor said into the phone.

Kate and Sandy looked at each other and raised their eyebrows. They both knew that Connor was upset.

He listened for a moment. "I don't care about

the written confession," Connor said. "Logan Sawyer, the older son, already tried that trick with Kate and me. I have copies of Cole's handwriting and that letter simply doesn't match. Furthermore … no, you listen to me!" Connor raised his voice. "Logan was written out of his father's will a month before the shooting and fire occurred."

Connor stopped talking and listened.

"FINE!" he yelled and slammed down the phone.

The two women looked to Connor for an update.

"What did she say?" asked Kate.

"He'll be arraigned before Judge Madison tomorrow morning at eight o'clock. He'll decide on bail."

"Charges? Kate asked

"First-degree murder, two counts, and arson," Connor answered.

"Oh, great! I knew I shouldn't have helped you!" Maggie said. She stormed out of the police department.

"Okay, let's see if we can at least manage to get him in an isolated cell," Connor said. Kate and Sundae followed him down the hall.

"We need a warrant for those university school

papers to show the difference in handwriting," Connor said to Kate. "You get to work on that so we can get them into Madison's hands before Cole's arraignment tomorrow. I'll work on the cell issue." He walked quickly, with Sundae trotting behind him.

---

Returning home, Maggie slammed the door from the garage into the kitchen with a resounding thud, rattling the collection of plates that hung on the wall. She headed straight for her laptop on the kitchen table and Googled "Innocence Project." Maggie had heard about them from a colleague at work. Once she found a contact number, she grabbed her cellphone and dialed. She left a message with the receptionist to have an attorney call her as soon as possible.

Then she hung up and turned on the TV in the living room. Candy Martin stood outside the Lakewood Police Department, using the front door as a backdrop. Holding a microphone, Candy waited for the cameras to focus on her before speaking.

"Today, the state police have arrested Cole Sawyer, eighteen, of Lakewood in the double homicide of his elderly father, Joel Sawyer, and friend, Fletcher Potts of Lakewood."

With that, the station switched to video of the house fire. Maggie switched off her TV and threw the remote on the end table.

---

Kate's phone rang. She looked at the caller ID and saw that it was Jimmy Potts. With the media trucks outside the police station, Kate knew that Jimmy had probably seen the news and was calling about that. Nevertheless, she had to get the warrant signed by a judge if she could. The clock was ticking on Cole's arraignment and Kate had to do whatever she could to get the judge to sign off on it. She made a mental note to call Jimmy as soon as she could.

---

As Connor walked by Sandy's office on the way to the jail cells, he stuck his head in the doorway.

"Sandy, would you please call Beth Ellis and ask her to come down here? Tell her they just arrested

Cole and we need her. Any word from Kate on the warrant?"

"I'll call Beth. Kate is still on her way to see if she can get the warrant from the judge. You know how traffic is at lunchtime.'

"I do. Can you text me as soon as you hear from Kate?"

"Will do."

CHAPTER 19

Connor convinced the guard to move Cole into a small cell that would isolate him from the general male population. He found Cole sitting on the narrow bed, rocking back and forth. Sundae jumped up on the bed and lay down next to Cole's leg, putting her head on his thigh. Cole stopped rocking and began gently petting Sundae's head. She always knew what was needed, Connor thought. The little beagle was so intelligent.

"Cole, I brought you a notebook. I'm sorry but the only thing they would allow me to bring you to write with is this box of Crayola crayons. At least it's a sixty-four count. If you use up one color, you have more," Connor said, hoping for some type of acknowledgment.

Cole refused to look at him, instead staring down at the floor. Connor set the crayons and note pad on the bed next to him. He noticed the red marks on Cole's wrist from the handcuffs.

"Cole, we really need to talk," Connor said.

Sitting on the foot of the bed, Cole made no effort to pick up the notebook or crayons to write. He was shutting down to the outside world, and that included Connor.

Connor looked up when he heard footsteps outside the cell door. A guard and Beth were standing there.

"I'll be back," Connor said as he went to the door to meet Beth.

"Your dog," the jailer said.

"Let her stay with him. She calms him."

The guard gave Connor a harsh look. "But policy…"

"I said let her stay there. She won't help him escape, trust me." Connor was beyond frustrated with everyone.

Beth and Connor went upstairs to his desk to talk.

"What the hell happened that they arrested him?" Beth asked.

"Logan's bogus confession letter didn't get the

desired response from Kate and me, so we think he somehow got it to the DA's office."

Beth thought for a minute. "What can I do to help?"

"I figured Cole would be upset but he won't even write on the pad or look at me. All he'll do is pet Sundae. We need to talk to him. He has to communicate. He'll be arraigned tomorrow morning. Can you try to get him to open up?"

Beth stood and began walking back to the guard's station. Connor followed her.

---

Kate watched Judge Madison look over the copies of Cole's schoolwork, then back to the bogus confession letter. The judge let out an audible sigh and returned to the pages of schoolwork.

"Detective … I simply…"

"Your honor," Kate interrupted. "Please. The older son tried to introduce another confession letter to us, about a week ago, which he said his adopted brother, Cole Sawyer, wrote. We obtained Cole Sawyer's handwriting samples from his school. We even had the FBI look over the two pieces of evidence. They said it wasn't a match. Please," Kate pleaded.

"Detective…

"I'm sorry, your honor."

The judge looked carefully at the evidence again. He leaned back in his leather chair and looked up at the ceiling in thought. Kate knew better than to say another word. She'd made her case and now said a silent prayer as she waited.

---

Beth stepped into the cell and Connor tried to follow. The jailer put his hand on Connor's chest, stopping him.

"One person at a time."

Connor was about to lose his temper, then decided against it.

"I'll be down the hallway," Connor said.

Beth sat on Cole's bed and greeted Sundae.

"Cole, my name is Beth Ellis. I want to help you but you also have to help me. I'll need you to please write some answers."

Beth reached out and touched the red marks on Cole's wrists. Cole quickly jerked his arm away from Beth.

"Does that hurt? Can I get you anything for the marks on your wrists?"

Cole looked at the floor and refused to write anything.

"Do you like Sundae? She's so sweet. Aren't her ears soft?" Beth said, trying a different approach.

Still nothing. The boy had shut down.

"Cole, I'll leave my number with the guard. If you want to talk to me, I'll come back. Any time, night or day. But Cole, you'll be meeting with a judge tomorrow and you'll need to write your answers for him."

Beth stood up, patted Sundae one more time, and called to be let out of the cell. The guard let her out, then closed and relocked the door with a thud that made Cole jump.

---

Detectives Barton and Harris stepped into the small bar on Second Street. The place smelled of booze, pot, and urine. It was a real dump, even for a bar, Bob thought. Harris pulled out a chair, as did Barton.

They had followed Logan here. Their table was off to the right and back from where he was sitting.

Logan ordered what looked like a whiskey and, with a pull of courage, downed it in one gulp. Then he got up and walked to a payphone on the wall by the bathrooms. Bob rose and slowly strolled toward him, trying to listen. He heard Logan ask to speak to Candy Martin. Bob knew she was the TV news reporter who always managed to get under Connor's skin. He lingered in the hallway, jingling the change in his pocket as if he were waiting to use the phone.

"Why don't you take a hike?" Logan snarled at Bob.

"I need to call my wife. To pick me up. I had too much to drink," Bob said, thinking that was as good an excuse as any to be hanging around the payphone. He staggered, swayed a little, and leaned against the wall to put the finishing touches on his act.

When the receptionist at the TV station was unable to reach Candy, she must have told Logan that he could leave a message for her. Logan said he would call back. Bob assumed that Logan didn't want Candy to know his identity. Also, Bob could clearly see the outline of Logan's cell phone, which was tucked into the front pocket of his expensive slacks.

"All yours, buddy." Logan turned to Bob and hung up the phone.

Logan walked back, tossed a bill on the table, and strolled out the door. Quickly, Bob returned to their table.

"Let's go. He was trying to get in touch with Candy Martin. As soon as we get in the car, text Connor and Kate and let them know," Bob said.

At the same time, Connor sent a text to Kate. When she didn't answer, he hit her number on speed dial.

"Kate Stroup," she answered.

"Did you get the judge to sign the warrant?"

CHAPTER 20

"All rise. This court is now in session."

The Honorable Judge Madison strolled to the bench in his black robe. He glanced over the morning docket and nodded at the bailiff to call the first case. Cole's arraignment was the third on the docket. Connor, Kate, and Beth sat on the right side of the courtroom. Maggie sat on the opposite side, refusing to sit or speak to any of them.

"I wonder who that young man in the suit is, the one sitting next to Maggie," Kate whispered to Connor.

Connor turned and glanced in Maggie's direction.

After the first two cases were heard, Cole was

brought in. He wore an orange jumpsuit and was visibly frightened and shaking. He never looked up from the table in front of him. The judge was reading the paperwork on the case. Judge Madison adjusted his glasses and looked out, searching the courtroom. He called over the bailiff and the two whispered something that no one could hear. The bailiff shook his head.

"Who is representing Mr. Sawyer?" the judge asked in his baritone voice, not seeing the public defender sitting next to Cole.

"I am, your honor." The man sitting next to Maggie stood up.

"Approach the bench, son. I don't think I've ever seen you in my courtroom."

The young man approached the bench, spoke with the judge for a few minutes, then returned to his seat next to Cole.

"The court will recognize attorney Judd Dale, the defendant's counsel," Judge Madison announced.

Attorney Judd Dale was a friend of Maggie's who had worked with the Innocence Project at one time.

"You gotta be kidding me," a voice said from the back of the courtroom.

"I'll have no outbursts in my courtroom. Is that understood?" Judge Madison said in an authoritative voice.

Kate turned but, from her position, couldn't see who had made the comment. The prosecutor, sitting at the table opposite from Cole, shook his head and sent his assistant scrambling out of the courtroom. Connor figured it was to find out just who this attorney was. As Connor watched the assistant leave, he saw Logan sitting in the back of the courtroom.

"Looks like Logan wanted a first-hand account of what's going to happen to his adopted brother. I wondered who made that comment," Connor whispered in Kate's ear.

"Gentlemen, please approach the bench," Judge Madison bellowed.

Both the defense and prosecuting attorneys approached the bench. The judge handed a copy of the handwriting from the confession letter and Cole's schoolwork, along with the FBI's comparison notes of the two documents, to each attorney. Cole's attorney studied the comparison notes, then glanced at the handwriting of both the letter and the schoolwork.

"Your honor..." Attorney Dale said.

"Mr. Dale, I'm well aware of what you're about to say. Given the fact that the prosecuting attorney is just now seeing this, I'd like to allow forty-eight hours for both sides to review.

"Your Honor, I'd like the court to allow bail for my client. He can't drive, he's mute, and I hardly believe he's a flight risk," Attorney Dale said.

"Your Honor," the prosecutor protested.

"Counselor, please, allow me to speak. First, I have to agree with Mr. Dale that Mr. Sawyer is hardly a flight risk. Given the fact that neither of you has seen these documents until today, and that you need to thoroughly examine them, I'd like to grant bail to Mr. Sawyer while you do just that." The judge peered over the top of his glasses at both attorneys.

---

The former Innocence Project lawyer was able to get bail set low enough that Maggie could put up her house as collateral. Logan Sawyer was noticeably upset at the judge's decision and stormed out of the courtroom. In the lobby, he kicked a trash can. It tipped over, spilling its contents on the floor as it rolled.

Bob and Grant saw this and tailed his every move as he left the courthouse parking lot.

Connor and Kate walked over to Maggie while she waited for Cole's release and the attorney.

"Maggie, I know you're upset with us over Cole's arrest. Please understand that we had nothing to do with it. It was the DA's office that made this decision, not the Lakewood Police Department," Connor said.

Maggie folded her arms in front of her like a drill sergeant and said nothing.

"Maggie, please. We can win this only by working together," Kate said, reaching out and rubbing Maggie's forearm softly. "We don't believe Cole killed his father. We're all on the same side. While we can't go into the details of an ongoing investigation, I can tell you that we're watching another person."

"Maggie, I have to go. I need to get Sundae. She stayed with Cole last night," Connor said as he left the two women to talk.

"Maggie, Connor slept in his office last night, checking on Sundae and Cole throughout the night. As he said, Sundae spent the night in jail with Cole for his protection. Connor had to feed and water her but was forced to bring in a collapsible rubber bowl for her water. Her stainless-steel bowl wasn't allowed even though Connor is a detective. Connor brought in a bed but Sundae never left Cole's side. Connor checked on both of them several times during the night," Kate said.

Connor came back with Sundae by his side. "I need to go home and take a shower before we start work," Connor said, looking at Kate.

As they turned to leave, Maggie touched them both on the arm.

"I'm sorry for lashing out at the two of you yesterday. I've put in so many hours working with Cole. I know in my heart he couldn't do this." Tears spilled over and rolled down her cheeks. "I want what's best for him and I honestly felt that once Joel and his wife adopted him, he finally had just that. Until this."

Maggie fought back more tears, knowing the journey to Cole's innocence was a long way off.

Kate reached over and hugged Maggie.

"Cole is lucky he has you," Kate said.

"Maggie, I'm going to request that a unit watch your house. This isn't because we're watching Cole or you. I'd just feel better, as whoever wrote that bogus confession letter may not be too happy that Cole has been released on bail," Connor said.

Maggie looked at Connor with a worried expression. "Are we in any danger?" she asked.

"I don't think so, but I don't want to take any chances with your or Cole's well-being."

---

Connor, Kate, and Sundae stopped by the dispatch desk.

"Sandy, I'm going home to take a shower. Kate will be on call with my car once she drops me off at the house," Connor said.

Sandy nodded as she wrote down the information that was coming in from a call on the 911 line.

"Think I'll throw you in the shower with me, you little jailbird," Connor said, petting Sundae as they walked to their police unit.

Connor's cell phone chimed. It was Grant Harris.

"Maxwell." Connor listened for a few minutes. "On our way." He disconnected the call. "Shower will have to wait," Connor said, looking at Sundae. "Kate, radio Sandy. Tell her we're en route to Shelton Law Office. Barton and Harris just called, saying that Logan went in like a madman."

Kate's phone chimed with a text from Abigail. It

read, "Hurry, please! Logan is here. He pulled the attorney into his office and slammed the door. I called 911 but I'm scared. Logan is out of control."

CHAPTER 21

*A*bigail stood next to her car in the parking lot of Shelton Law. Even from a distance, Connor and Kate could see that she was visibly shaking. They stopped their car in front of hers. Bob and Grant's unmarked car was parked down the street, out of sight, as they didn't want to blow their cover.

Connor, Kate, and Sundae jumped out of the car.

"He's a crazy man!" Abigail cried, dabbing her eyes with a wadded-up tissue. "He's totally out of control again. He burst into the office, demanding to speak with Attorney Shelton. I told him he was on a call with another client. He refused to listen. I think he was high again. He ran down the hallway like a madman. I tried to stop him but he hit me and pushed me down. He kept saying, 'I want my money from my dad's estate. It's mine, not his!' He wouldn't listen to me and just went into Mr. Shelton's office, slammed the door, and locked it. I heard yelling and then what sounded like furniture being thrown around. I called 911 and texted you."

---

"Stay here with Abigail. I'll go in," Connor told Kate.

He and Sundae approached the office. As Connor entered, he looked down the long hallway. At the end was a metal door standing partly open. Connor could see the back parking lot through it.

"Logan!" Connor called out but heard nothing. Slowly, he and Sundae crept down the hallway. "Mr. Shelton," Connor called.

The door to Mr. Shelton's office was ajar. Connor opened it and found the attorney on the floor. His tie was pulled to one side, his suit jacket was torn, and blood spattered his white shirt. Connor could see that the attorney had suffered a head wound from his encounter with Logan. He checked for a pulse, then hit the speed dial for Kate.

"Get an ambulance. The office is clear. I'm going out the back door. It was left open."

Kate and Abigail rushed in as Kate called to request an ambulance, then checked for a pulse.

"He's still breathing," Kate said, looking up at Abigail. Kate glanced around the office. Papers littered the floor and the file cabinet drawers had all been pulled open.

Connor looked down the alley behind the law office, where there were trash cans and marked parking slots for each office suite. Sundae searched around the parked cars as Connor dialed Bob.

"Did you see him leave?"

"No. He parked in that little strip mall down the road and walked in the front door. Why?" Bob asked.

"He's gone. Must've left out the back door behind the office. Tore up the office pretty good. The attorney is on the floor, knocked out cold. We have an ambulance en route," Connor said.

"Grant and I will get back to the strip mall and see if we can find him."

Bob and Grant ran back to their unmarked car and headed directly to the mall.

"There." Grant pointed.

Logan's BMW sped away from the strip mall but not before hitting a lone shopping cart, sending it rolling across the parking lot until it hit the rear quarter panel of a newer Camaro. The car's alarm system sounded.

"92, PD, be advised that we're in pursuit of a BMW i8 Coupe heading northbound on Roma," Bob radioed to Lakewood Police dispatch. He engaged the light bar on the front grill of the car and Grant flipped the switch on the siren.

"10.4, 92," the Lakewood dispatcher said. "He's up there." Grant pointed toward the

BMW weaving in and out of the vehicles four car lengths in front of them.

Bob pulled behind an old silver Buick. A white-haired man was driving ten miles under the speed limit, with his hands at ten and two on the steering wheel. Up ahead, a chorus of horns blared. Logan's car veered into the oncoming lane of traffic. Cars and trucks moved as far as possible to get out of his way, their tires sending up clouds of dust and gravel from the shoulder.

"Come on, pull over and get out of my way!"

Bob said as he pounded his fist on the steering wheel. "It's times like this I wish I had a horn that sounded like a shotgun blast!"

A steady stream of cars passed them in the oncoming lane. The man driving in front refused to pull out of their way.

Grant removed the microphone from its holder on the dashboard and flipped on the car's PA.

"Driver in the silver Buick, pull over!"

When the driver still refused to pull over, Grant turned up the volume.

"Pull over NOW!"

As if a light bulb suddenly went on in the old man's head, he slowly pulled over to the shoulder and out of their way. As Bob and Grant passed by, the old man flipped them off.

"I can't believe it. Did you see what that old fart did?" Bob asked.

"Yeah, but now I've lost sight of Logan's car," Grant said.

Bob continued running code until they passed by Broadway and Roma.

"He must have taken one of the intersections up to the freeway," Bob said.

"95, PD, we lost the subject."

"127, 95, a BMW just got on I-25 heading

south. I'm trying to catch up to him. He's traveling at a high speed."

The patrolman's siren could be heard wailing in the background over his open mic.

"15 and 49, we're all cleared from the last call. PD, we'll be heading southbound on I-25. Be advised that the ambulance has taken Attorney Shelton to Lakewood Hospital. We need a uniform to go over there to take a statement from his assistant. She followed the ambulance to the hospital," Connor said.

Kate's cell phone rang. She answered without looking at it. "Stroup… What? Ace, I can't talk to you right now," she said and disconnected the call.

"Ace? Wanting money again?" Connor asked, glancing at Kate.

"Hell, I have no idea what he wants. He came over the other night and said WE needed to talk. He ate one of my hamburgers and fries until I showed him to the door," Kate said.

The police radio interrupted their conversation. "127, PD, be advised, I'm losing him. Whatever that BMW has under the hood, he's got a lot more horses than I do. He's weaving in and out of traffic, running people off the road.

"15, PD, do we have a state police officer anywhere close to 127's location?"

"PD, 127, what's your mile marker?" the dispatcher asked.

"Stand by ... marker 144, PD," the uniformed officer answered.

"Negative, SP is at least 20 minutes away," the dispatcher reported.

"15, 127, can you see him at all?" Connor asked.

"Negative. Once he went over that hill outside of the city limits, he was gone. I looked for dust clouds off the freeway in case he took off down a side road, but didn't see any," the patrolman radioed back.

"It's over, ladies and gentlemen. Pull back," Connor said to the other officers.

They were well out of their jurisdiction, and without even a glimpse of Logan's car, the chase was futile not to mention dangerous to other drivers on the road.

"15, PD, ask Sandy to pull all the information on Logan Sawyer's car, a complete description, and get out a BOLO on that car as well as the driver, Logan Sawyer," Connor radioed back.

CHAPTER 22

After Cole's release from jail, Maggie kept a watchful eye on him. Between losing his father in the fire and being arrested for something she knew he hadn't done, the young man had been through a lot. After several days, she thought she should take him to school, to get him back into his routine. However, when she consulted Connor and Kate, they advised against it, at least until they could find Logan.

In the short time he had lived with Maggie, Cole had read all seventy-five books on her bookshelf but refused to write anything in response to any questions asked of him. Beth Ellis visited Cole but was unable to unlock the written voice within the boy. Judd Dale, the attorney, tried several times to talk with Cole to prepare for his case. However, Cole refused to respond to any of his questions.

Connor and Kate dropped by to bring more books for Cole to read and math puzzle books for him to complete. Sundae ran back to the room where Cole was staying and jumped on the bed. Cole sat petting her, so Connor decided to leave Sundae with him a couple of hours a day. Maggie marveled at the healing effect the little beagle had on Cole. If only Sundae could talk to Cole and get him to respond to her. Maybe in her own way she was, Maggie thought to herself. Maggie was worried as she looked at the untouched math puzzle books. The stack was growing. Cole's homework, which had been sent home, sat next to them. That, too, was untouched.

The puzzles and homework were left unsolved and answers remained locked within Cole's mind.

Logan drove the BMW beyond the county line, turned down a deserted road, and pulled off into some brush. He broke branches and did his best to cover up his car. Once he was satisfied, he pulled out his burner phone and called a friend to pick him up.

Abigail sat in the box at the Lakewood Police Department. The bluish-purple marks that Logan's attack had left on her wrist and forearm were more visible today than they'd been on the day of the altercation at Shelton Law Firm. Kate knew all too well that the worst damage at the hands of an abusive man was on the inside and couldn't be seen.

"How is Mr. Shelton doing?" asked Kate.

"Not good. He's still in a coma. I was in last night and the doctor told me he has a lot of swelling in the brain."

Abigail dabbed at a tear. Kate reached out and touched her forearm.

"I know this has to be hard on you," Connor said.

"I've spent the last few days trying my best to put paperwork back into files and cancel client appointments. One of John's friends called and volunteered to come in a few hours a week to work on pending cases," Abigail said.

Connor noted it was the first time he'd heard Abigail refer to the attorney by his first name.

"Abigail, we asked you to come in today to help us understand Logan better," Connor said.

"Detective Maxwell, I think you'd need a shrink to do that."

The three of them laughed.

"I was hoping you could fill in some blanks for us. His friends, favorite places to go, things like that," Connor said.

Abigail thought about the question before answering.

"I went to high school with Logan. He was always playing Mr. Tough Guy, the bully … you know. When we got together in high school, he seemed to calm down. At least for a time."

"And what changed?" Kate asked as she tucked a strand of hair behind her ear.

Abigail sighed heavily. "He got in with this group of guys. Some were still in high school, others were older. They picked on Cole and this Jewish boy in school. They thought they were better than them. A black family moved into the Lakewood area and they picked on the son, too. One day, they found the black boy on the football field. He'd been badly beaten. No one was ever arrested.

"Logan told me he was a member of some group. He never explained who was in it or what the group was. About six months later, a boy 'came out of the closet' and Logan and the guys picked on him. The boy was found tied to a barbwire fence, beaten to death. They never found out who did it. It was around that time that I got a weird feeling about Logan."

"Can you explain the feeling?" Connor asked.

"Not really. I mean, I still cared for him but I didn't feel safe around him. I guess I always wondered if he and his friends were behind some of the hate crimes. I broke it off with him. When we got together later in life, I thought he had changed but by now he was into drugs and all types of weird stuff, which he kept hidden from me for a while. I told you it was the drugs that broke us up but it was more than that."

"What was it?" Connor asked.

Abigail bit her lower lip and looked down at the metal table, then back at Connor.

"It was the men he was hanging out with. I knew they had meetings and no one except them was allowed to attend. Some of the guys that Logan hung around with in high school were in this group. Logan started buying weapons and going out to target practice."

"Was it like a gun club?" Kate asked.

"No, they'd go to a member's ranch outside the city limits. If the head guy told them something, they'd all believe it and follow his orders. It sounded like they were being brainwashed, honestly. He'd tell me the weirdest things and when I didn't buy into it, he'd get upset with me." Abigail took a sip of water from the bottle in front of her.

Kate wrote down everything.

"Abigail, did Logan ever mention the name of the group?" Connor asked.

"No."

Connor was already formulating an idea. He had heard from one of the deputies, Pat Davis at the Natick Sheriff's Department, that there was a group of men in the county who hung out at an old ranch. The place was close to seventy-five acres, fully fenced and gated. The neighbors had mentioned seeing old military surplus being hauled in by truck. One day, Abe Harley, a rancher whose fence line bordered the place, was looking over his cattle with his drone. He happened to get a little nosey and saw men going through what looked like some type of military training or exercise.

He called Pat out and told him about the military surplus being brought into the old ranch, then showed Pat the training footage his drone had captured. In this post-9/11 era, Abe felt it was his civic duty to report it to the police. As they say: *"If you see something, say something."* Connor had driven by the ranch many times on his way to go hiking and always wondered why the place had an eight-foot-tall fence topped with razor wire. A large metal gate was always locked and had a box, which he assumed was for security, requiring a key card or security personnel to allow people in or out. Signs were posted every few feet, warning, in large block letters: "NO TRESPASSING ELECTRIC FENCE."

---

Logan walked out through the wooded area and toward the highway. He hid in the tree-lined area beside the road until an old-style military jeep pulled off the road and honked three times.

"Take me to the ranch," Logan said as he hopped into the jeep. The driver pulled onto the highway.

CHAPTER 23

The day started at seven o'clock with Connor dropping off Carlos and Pebbles at their tracking class. He knew the two would be there the better part of the day. Carlos was so excited about his tracking class with his little beagle. He wanted to be just like Connor. His goal was to join the Lakewood Police Department as soon as he could. While Connor was thrilled the boy looked up to him, he also knew that Carlos' choices at this age could change like the weather.

Kate had made plans to pick up Jimmy Potts, who was wheelchair-bound, to make funeral arrangements for his brother, Fletcher. The charred remains of Fletcher Potts had been released by the ME's office to the funeral home on Thursday. When

Kate heard this, she called and volunteered to drive Jimmy over.

Connor decided to go hiking in the hills surrounding Lakewood. It was his day off and a good way to wick away the stress of the workweek. He drove beyond the city limits and observed as the businesses of Lakewood were replaced by fence-lined pastures where cattle lazily grazed, or where fields of alfalfa or sorghum grew.

He'd been following the white ribbons painted on the asphalt for miles when he saw the first signs of the highly secured ranch stretching out before him. Reducing his speed, he looked over the layout and wondered what was really going on beyond the locked gate and the miles of electrified fencing. Two men wearing camouflage uniforms were driving a four-seater ATV along the inside fence line of the ranch. It was also decked out in camouflage paint. Connor slowed his truck and watched the men in his rearview mirror for as long as he could without being noticed.

Once they were out of sight, he returned to the posted speed limit and continued. Within ten minutes, he had reached the trailhead of the mountains, where he grabbed his backpack. Sundae jumped out and followed him up the trail. Connor glanced toward the far north side of the mountain and decided to explore that part of the range. He could see that the narrow trail was less traveled, as it was barely visible and covered in brush. He began his ascent with Sundae by his side.

---

Kate and Jimmy sat in the funeral director's small office. Kate thought the gray paint on the wall was as depressing as going into the place itself. Jimmy looked through a catalog featuring caskets of all models and prices in the first half, and urns of all sizes and shapes in the second half. Kate could see that the stress of making these final decisions was weighing heavily on Jimmy's mind.

"Did Fletcher ever mention his wishes to you, what he wanted?' Kate asked Jimmy.

"No, we never talked about it. I think we both thought I'd go first," Jimmy answered.

"He lost his wife several years ago. Was she buried or cremated?" Kate asked, thinking that might help Jimmy decide.

"She was cremated. However, my brother was Catholic. She wasn't."

Just then, the door opened and the funeral director, predictably dressed in a black suit, entered. He carried a file folder. The smell of flowers from the chapel wafted in behind him.

"My name is Adam Laufer. I worked with your brother when your sister-in-law passed. Your brother made all the arrangements for his own funeral at that time. In fact, everything is paid for as well."

Jimmy breathed a sigh of relief, especially after having seen the prices of the caskets.

The funeral director opened the file. "I'm sorry for the wait but I had to find the file. Seems your brother is Catholic and wants to be buried in Sunset Park. Your sister-in-law's urn will be placed with him in the same plot, which has also been taken care of. Fletcher paid for a double headstone for both of their names," Adam stated.

"I'm sorry, I probably shouldn't butt in. However, Jimmy's brother died in a house fire. If the funeral home didn't keep the ashes, they're probably gone," Kate said.

The funeral director quickly looked through the file, tapping the end of his pen on the desk as he turned the pages.

"We do sell some metal urns. Maybe…" Adam trailed off as he looked through the paperwork.

"No, it appears Mr. Potts chose a simple wooden box for the remains of his wife and took possession of her ashes."

Silence reigned as Jimmy thought about what he should do.

"Would he have put the ashes in a safety deposit box?" Kate asked.

"I don't know if he had one," Jimmy answered.

"If he had one, it would probably be where he banked. If you know that, I can call them and take you over."

Kate reached over and handed Jimmy a tissue as tears formed in the elderly man's eyes and began to roll down his cheek.

"If the ashes were only in a wooden box, the box was probably burned in the fire," Jimmy said, distraught.

"Often, people accept the ashes of a departed loved one in a less expensive box until they feel up to choosing something more appropriate. Do you know if they found a metal urn after the fire?" the funeral director asked.

Kate shook her head no. "Jimmy, why don't I take you home? It seems everything is taken care of here. You've gone through a lot today. We can stop on our way and get some lunch. My treat," Kate said as she stood and took the handles of the wheelchair.

"I'll call you later with some dates and times to arrange your brother's memorial service," Adam said.

Jimmy just nodded.

---

It took Connor the better part of the morning to reach the top of the north ridge. He looked around. It was majestical, standing on the highest peak of a mountain that he loved. The fresh air and the sound of a light breeze blowing through the trees made a music all their own. Connor closed his eyes for a moment to take it all in. Looking down, being able to see for miles, he imagined that this must be what heaven was like. He knew it must be beautiful.

Connor turned around and sat on a large boulder. He pulled off his backpack and got Sundae's travel bowl and water. Connor ate a sandwich and drank some water out of his bottle. He gave Sundae her snacks, then pulled out his binoculars. He swept his gaze across the desert floor below him.

He'd never found Mia Gordon's body. She was a young dental assistant who had worked with her father. She'd been abducted and Connor and Kate had worked her case years ago. The fact that they'd never found her body haunted Connor. He'd never stopped looking for her, telling himself he had to do it so her father could finally put closure to the tragedy. Connor knew that he had to do it for the victim as well. That was just the type of detective he was.

From atop the northside of the mountain, he looked for any earth that seemed to have been recently disturbed but found nothing, nor any skeletal remains. He saw a jackrabbit run from one sagebrush to another and a tumbleweed dance across the desert floor below him. Understanding the killer as he did, Connor knew that he never buried his victims. He would simply discard them like trash.

Next, Connor trained his binoculars in the direction of the ranch but the distance was simply too far for him to make out what was going on. He wondered if Logan was hiding within the confines of that ranch. Was that the place Abigail was describing?

He made a mental note to call his buddy at the Natick Sheriff's Department when he got back down the mountain.

"If only we had a drone. We might be able to see if Logan is hiding out at that ranch down there," Connor said to Sundae as she wagged her tail.

Connor lay back against the boulder, using his backpack as a pillow. Sundae curled up beside him. He looked up into the sky and studied the vastness of God's blue canvas above him. He watched God's paintbrush strokes as He painted the cumulus clouds into shapes slowly drifting overhead. Connor reached over and pet Sundae as she put her head on his stomach.

The radiant heat from the morning sun had baked the boulder with its warmth and it felt good on Connor's back. A light breeze danced across his face and dark brown hair. His eyelids became heavy as the stress of the workweek drained from him and he dozed off to sleep.

CHAPTER 24

Logan swaggered into the office, which was lit only by two dim sconces on the dark wood wall behind the desk. Twin computer screens cast an eerie blueish glow on the large man sitting behind the desk. Bill Kingston, aka The King, was waiting for Logan. For several years now, The King had been the head of a local group at the ranch, called The Brotherhood. His rolled-up sleeves exposed several tats depicting the American flag, clenched fists, and a swastika. The King was six foot three and was made of the large, knotted muscles that came from steroid use and plain craziness. His head and body were devoid of hair.

"Sit," The King commanded in his deep voice.

Logan took a seat in the leather-backed chair across from the desk.

"They released Cole, that ... RETARD ... on bail. That stupid bitch, his old social worker, put her house up for collateral. He's out pending trial," Logan said.

The King allowed his twisted mind to contemplate this for a minute.

"And you can't get your hands on any of your inheritance money?"

"No, I tried. That stupid attorney told me no. All of my father's money is locked up in a trust. Anyway, that's what he told me."

"I heard you almost killed the asshole attorney. It's all over the news. They're not sure he's going to make it. Not that the world needs another bleeding-heart attorney like him. He's a disgrace to our race. But why did you go in there with a witness? You'd have been better off if you could have done this clean, with no witness."

"I lost my temper. I just want what's mine. My father should have known better than to give that kid anything. Why should I share with a kid who's not even related to me? Then he changes his damn will and I find out the house I grew up in goes to Fletcher, his friend. When that old dude died, it would have gone to the little bastard that no one wanted ... except my father and mother. I HATE that kid. He'd been in foster home after foster home. Doesn't that tell you something? A reject, that's all he is. He isn't like you and me." Logan stood and started pacing back and forth.

"Stop!" The King bellowed. Logan stopped and took his seat.

"He should have D-I-E-D in that fire," Logan said.

"He didn't, so we need to get you out of here. The Brotherhood will transport you to another state, where you can stay with a member there. I'll talk to Chavez. He's a lawyer and has been with our group for several years. He can let me know what he can do in your defense. Of course, that will depend on whether your ex-girlfriend's boss lives or dies."

---

Connor met Deputy Patrick Davis of the Natick Sheriff Department at the adjoining ranch. The ranch, owned by Abe Harley, had been in the family for over one hundred years. The three men sat at a large oak dining table and Abe showed to Connor the video that his drone had captured. Connor watched the video while Abe made small talk with Deputy Davis.

Connor began watching the footage a second time.

"It looks like some military group. Anyway, that's what I first thought," Abe said. "They're all in uniforms but no US patches like when I was in boot camp or special training. The other thing I noticed and thought was odd is that they're all white men. No one of color."

"Does your drone make any noise? What I mean is, could you fly it again without them detecting it?" Connor asked.

"The old drones, I think, are right around eighty decibels," Deputy Davis said. "The department has one that I believe may be sixty decibels. We got it about a month ago. I can check with the pilot and see."

Connor knew normal traffic was about sixty decibels and had read that an average vacuum was around seventy-five. So, in Connor's mind, eighty was too loud to fly over the range, even at whatever height a drone could go.

"Would the SO allow us to use it? Connor asked.

"I can check and see."

"If Abe would allow us to come back out, we could act like we're checking on the herd of cattle," Connor said.

"Only one problem with that," Deputy Davis said.

"What's that?" Connor asked.

"I know ours has Sheriff's Department decals on both sides and the bottom," Deputy Davis said.

"What if I bought one myself? Could your pilot tell me what type to buy? If I request one for the department, with all the red tape, we may or may not get one. Or worse yet, it would take months," Connor said.

"Do you ever hear any odd noises coming from over there?" the deputy asked Abe.

"When they first took over that old ranch, there was a lot of construction noise. Looked like they build some big auditorium or something. Then there was all the military equipment being delivered. If I was headed to town, sometimes they'd tie up both traffic lanes getting into that locked gate with large trucks hauling equipment. At first, I assumed it was some type of military training facility. You know, like special training. It was obvious to me that it wasn't being used as a ranch anymore.

"One day, I was out on my four-wheeler,

checking my fence line, and ran into two men on the other side of the fence. They were on one of those real expensive four-wheelers that seat four people. They were armed and in uniforms with no troop numbers or any decals. I stopped and tried to talk to them. Those two weren't talkers. I asked what branch of the military they were in. They told me to mind my own business and then went on their way. Odd, I thought."

"Is that the only interaction you've had with them?" Connor asked.

"I've been missing calves, about one a month. At first, I thought it was coyotes. But you usually find the bones. I started checking my fences again and noticed that their large eight-foot electric fence had a make-shift gate that led into my property. At first glance, you wouldn't even notice it. But I looked it over and with the electricity turned off, they could enter my property. So, the next time I ran across them checking their fence line, I asked them if they knew about the area about two miles up from where we were, the area that looked like a gate. They said nothing. When I told them I'd been missing cattle, they just laughed at me and drove on. That was when I purchased my drone. Whenever I have cattle on that pasture next to them, I fly my drone as much as I can."

"Have you ever seen them trespassing on your property?" Deputy Davis asked.

"No. I purchased a few trail cams and put them on some fence posts," Abe said.

"And what happened?" Connor asked.

"They turned up missing," Abe said.

Connor thought for a few minutes.

"All pastureland out there, no buildings?" Connor asked.

"Nope," Abe answered.

"No sage?"

"Nope, just miles and miles of pastureland and fence. That's why I purchased the drone. But not knowing when they're taking the cattle is the problem."

"Branded?"

"Yep, got '3 H' on the left hip. That was my father's brand and when I took over the ranch, I renewed it in my name."

CHAPTER 25

Carlos' grandmother had made a full recovery from her heart attack and her doctors deemed her able to return home. Three times a week, home health care workers would stop by to check on her and her health. After work, Connor and Carlos opened up Nana's house and aired it out. They put clean sheets on Nana's bed and towels in the bathroom. Connor left Carlos at the house while he purchased basic groceries like milk, cereal, eggs, bread, and other things for Nana and Carlos.

Carlos was changing the sheets on his bed when Connor returned with the groceries All that was left for them to do was pick up Nana at the hospital.

The following morning, Connor and Sundae stood in the doorway of the former guestroom/junk room, which had been converted into Carlos' and Pebbles' bedroom while they stayed with him. The room was tidy and the bed made. The morning sun was just beginning to peek through the blinds, casting long rectangular lines of light and shadow on the hardwood floor.

"Just not the same around here, is it?"

Connor reached down and pet Sundae as he looked at the small desk he had purchased for Carlos to do his homework. The desk chair was pushed in, no backpack hung off the back of the chair, and no school books or papers littered the desk. Just a pencil holder with a few pens and pencils stood upright.

"We'd better get ready for work. It's just you and me today. Kate is taking Jimmy Potts to his brother's funeral."

Connor turned away from Carlos' bedroom but not before he started to close the door as he always had before Carlos came to live with him. He stopped himself and reopened the door.

It was 5:45 when the sun began its ascent over the mountains. A van rolled to a stop and a stocky, muscular man got out.

"You Logan Sawyer?" he asked.

"That would be me," Logan said, picking up a large duffle bag.

Logan and the stocky man drove through the gates of the ranch and headed toward I-25 North. The interstate had snow-covered shoulders and snaked around some sleepy northern towns. Four hours later, they crossed the Colorado border without having said a word to each other.

There, the desert stopped and tall trees began to dot the horizon along with snow-covered hills and mountains. Logan alternately dozed off and woke as the van approached the Kansas border.

"Hey, Dorothy, I got to gas up if you need to pee," the driver said, making reference to *The Wizard of Oz*. He pulled off the exit ramp and into a gas station, then stopped alongside a gas pump. The man went in, paid for fuel, and got some coffee. Logan used the restroom, then got coffee and two donuts. After the van was filled up, the two men were back on the road. The tires hummed away.

"So, I was wondering if you'd know anyone who could take care of some unfinished business for me," Logan said.

"What type of business would that be?" the man asked, glancing over at Logan.

"I need a guy picked up and brought to me. I'll pay," Logan said.

"Aah ... I see. Let me think about it."

The King had already left word with the Brotherhood that Logan may want to pick up his adopted brother and get rid of him. The word came down that no member was to get further involved in Logan's dealings with his younger brother.

Logan noticed the land becoming flatter as they drove. As the van headed east, he could see the large GPS screen tracking their path across the digital map on the van's dash.

"Where are you taking me?" Logan asked.

"I need to do another pickup in Kansas. Then we'll drop down to the bottom of the US and head to Florida. Did you bring your bathing suit and shades, Dorothy?"

Logan was getting pissed at the stocky guy referring to him as Dorothy. But the man stood at least six inches taller and weighed at least seventy-five pounds more than he did. Not to mention the dude was all muscle and looked like a linebacker with hands as big as dinner plates.

"Just sit back and enjoy the ride. I need to pick up my relief driver in a few minutes. Then you'll be heading to the Sunshine State, Dorothy," he said, grinning at Logan.

---

Abigail sat by her employer's bedside, gently holding John Shelton's bruised and battered hand. She had come to Lakewood Memorial Hospital each day since her ex-boyfriend had attacked the attorney. John's hands and face were covered with bruises and cuts—defensive wounds from trying to fend off Logan. Monitors beeped softly in the background as Abigail's eyes became heavy and she drifted off to sleep.

John's right fingers moved ever so slightly. When she felt the movement, Abigail opened her eyes wide. She sat, alert now, waiting to see if it happened again. His index finger twitched. This time, she was sure of what she'd felt. Abigail raced out of the hospital room and grabbed the first nurse she saw in the hallway.

"Come quick, he's moving," Abigail said, as if

they shouldn't wait one more minute or else his hand would stop.

The nurse rushed into the room, with Abigail close behind. The two stood waiting and watching as John's finger twitched again.

"I'll notify his nurse and doctor," the nurse said as she hurried out of the room.

---

"To what do I owe the honor?" Beth asked, looking up at Connor.

Connor sat on the leather loveseat in Beth's office as Sundae walked over to Beth.

"I need a favor."

"You know this is going to cost you," Beth joked. She raised her dark eyebrows, exposing her big brown eyes.

Connor leaned forward and looked at her. "So, what did you have in mind?"

"Oh … maybe lunch." Beth looked at the day planner on her desk. "And, what do you know, you're in luck today. I don't have anything penciled in for lunch."

"Lunch it is."

"Where's Kate today?" Beth came around her desk and took a chair across from Connor.

"She volunteered to take the brother of the victim to his funeral."

"Nice man. I felt so sorry for him, losing his brother that way. So, what is it you need?" Beth asked.

"I need a cell phone tracked. We have equipment but nothing like the FBI CAST unit."

CAST, which stood for Cellular Analysis Survey Team, was a special unit within the FBI that could track a cellular phone within twenty feet of its location. The Lakewood Police Department's equipment was able to tell only where a cell phone pinged off of, and Connor wanted Logan's exact location.

"Did you ask the FBI?" Beth asked.

"No, you know the feds never…"

Beth interrupted Connor. "I'll call a friend with CAST and see if he can be of any help. Now, where should we meet for lunch?" She smiled at Connor.

CHAPTER 26

ate carefully pushed Jimmy Potts' wheelchair through the doorway to an open four-top table at Dan's Coffee and Pastry. After pulling away a straight-back chair, she pushed the elderly man up to the table. Seeing Kate, Dan came over, smiling broadly, with his black apron wrapped tightly around his waist.

"New partner today?" Dan joked as he placed lunch menus in front of Kate and Jimmy.

"No. Connor is working and I took the day off," Kate answered with a big smile for Dan.

"She was so nice to drive me to my brother's funeral this morning," Jimmy added.

Dan hadn't expected that response and hesitated for a second, not sure how to respond. Finally, he said, "I'm sorry for your loss. I'll give you time to look over the menu. Then I'll be back to take your orders."

Kate smiled at Dan as he turned and walked back to the counter.

"Have you been here before, Jimmy?" Kate asked.

"No, I can't say that I have," Jimmy answered, looking around. "The food smells absolutely marvelous. Makes my mouth water just sitting here."

"I haven't found anything that isn't delicious," Kate said, turning her attention to her menu. "I think I'm going to have the smoked ham with swiss on a croissant and a mocha latte."

"That sounds good. I'll have the same, only does this place make regular coffee? I'm not into the fancy coffees," Jimmy said.

"I'm sure they do, but you have to save room for dessert. This is all my treat. Dan's desserts are simply out of this world," Kate said, waving Dan over to take their order.

Once Dan had left to prepare their food, Jimmy and Kate talked about Fletcher's memorial service and where the two of them had grown up. When their meals were served, Jimmy couldn't stop talking about how tasty the food and coffee were. As they talked, the bell chimed on the front door, announcing that another guest had arrived at Dan's. Kate didn't turn around until she felt a hand on her shoulder. She smiled and turned but the smile quickly faded.

"Got yourself a sugar daddy now, I see," Ace said. "Funny, I always had you pegged more for that cowboy you work with."

Kate stood up quickly and set her napkin on the table.

"Jimmy, will you excuse me for a minute?"

"Sure…" Jimmy said, confused as to who this rude man was.

Kate took Ace by the arm and went outside with him. "Ace, how DARE you come in here and make a statement like that…to a man you know nothing about! I knew you were a jerk but honestly…to insult that man, really, you've stooped lower than even I thought you could go! That man just buried his brother this morning. He had no way of getting to the funeral service, so I volunteered to drive him. I also asked him to lunch so that he would have someone to talk to afterward. Just go before I really lose my temper."

Ace stood there, at a loss for words, then turned and left.

---

Beth was already at the Lakota when Connor walked in. She looked up and waved Connor to the table.

"Been here long?" Connor asked.

"Got here about five minutes ago. I turned the request in to my friend at CAST. He told me that he would start working on it. Any more intel on Logan?

"Nothing."

Connor pulled out his cell phone, scrolled to a photo, and pushed the phone across the table to Beth.

"A drone?" Beth raised an eyebrow.

"Supposed to be here today. Gotta love online shopping," Connor said.

"Boys and their toys." Beth shook her head.

"Not a toy. There's a ranch outside the city limits and some weird shit is happening over there. I want the drone to see what all is going on."

"Weird?"

"Military equipment, training, but it's not military."

"Do you want me to run it by the bureau for you, see if they have anything on their radar about the group?" Beth asked.

"Not yet. With the Sheriff's Department's help, we're still attempting to see what's really happening. Could be nothing but a bunch of guys with paintball guns paying to play army."

Beth had known Connor for several years. She had been a profiler with the bureau when their paths serendipitously crossed. They had been working on a murder case. Connor was the lead detective at the Sheriff's Department at the time and Beth had been dispatched to help profile the killer.

Back then, Connor had recently gone through a divorce he really didn't want. He needed someone to talk to, outside of the officers he worked with. He'd confided in Beth that his wife had hated his work, the long hours, and the danger it put him in. His ex-wife wanted children, but with Connor's work, she was afraid that she would be raising a family by herself if anything happened to him. Eventually, she had an affair and ended the marriage.

Beth saw Connor as a broken man, waiting for his ex to return. He still loved his ex-wife and refused to date anyone else. Beth had been attracted to Connor but knew that his heart had no room for her when he was still so much in love with the ghost from his past.

When Beth decided to leave the bureau, she chose to settle down in Lakewood, where the bureau had stationed her. She liked the area and the people, so she purchased a home and opened her own office as a private consultant for police departments around the southwest. She had worked with Connor on several cases but they'd never had anything but a professional relationship. Connor had finally moved on from his past. Beth always wondered if his ex-wife getting remarried, and then pregnant, had pushed Connor in that direction.

Connor also had an ex-girlfriend, Sofie. Sofie worked at Beth's dentist's office in Lakewood. Beth knew Sofie from her visits to the dentist. From time to time, Sofie would ask about Connor, knowing that he and Beth sometimes worked together. Beth's take was that Sofie still loved Connor but Connor no longer felt the same way.

Then there was Connor's partner, Kate. Beth had seen how Kate looked at Connor, and she knew that Kate had feelings for him. Not knowing what was going to happen between those two, Beth kept her feelings to herself out of respect for Kate

---

Logan had been at the Florida Brotherhood compound for just over a week. Restless and bored, he ventured out to the beaches on several occasions, and a few bars. With so many tourists in the area, Logan's logic was that he was just another face in a sea of people. It was late one Saturday night when he got to talking with a dude who Logan thought had spent a few too many days on the beach. His skin was so dark and cracked from the sun that Logan thought to himself he could be a walking poster for skin cancer.

They were making small talk at the Clam Shell, a dark and dingy bar off the tourist path. Soon, Logan thought about how this man could help him with a problem—the problem being his adopted brother, Cole. Logan bought the tanned guy another whiskey, the third in a row, and the guy loosened up. When Logan asked what he did for a living, the man said he was a kind of go-between who could set people up with whatever they needed.

"You know what I mean?" the dude asked, slurring.

"You mean drugs?" Logan asked.

While he was interested in drugs, they weren't Logan's main concern right now.

"Nah, man, anything…."

"Anything?" Logan asked.

CHAPTER 27

It was two o'clock in the morning before Logan wandered back to the Brotherhood compound through the hot and humid night air. The compound was laid out on two hundred sprawling acres hidden by a Florida forest of oak and pine trees. In the center was a clearing where the compound sat surrounded by the majestic trees. Several large buildings dotted the property, but for years, ever since the land was purchased, no one except the Brotherhood had known what sat there.

Logan was tired after his night of drinking at the Clam Shell. He went straight to the head, then to his room. He threw back the covers, unbuckled his belt, slipped off his jeans, and climbed into bed. Within minutes, he drifted off into a deep sleep. His restful state didn't last long. He began tossing and turning as his mind journeyed into a dream-like state.

Logan was standing on the back porch of his father's home when he heard footsteps approaching from behind. Turning quickly, he saw his father, Joel Sawyer, facing him.

"Why?" Joel asked, looking his son straight in the eyes. Smoke billowed out of his mouth as he spoke.

Logan choked on the smoke and ran, stopping only when his father blocked his path.

"Why?" his father repeated as he reached out a charred hand toward him.

Logan's heart pounded and his head throbbed as he ran away from his father.

"No, no, get away from me! You're dead. You can't be here!"

Logan skidded to a stop. This time, Fletcher Potts stood blocking his path.

"Why?" asked Fletcher, with smoke seeping through his burned lips.

"No, get AWAY from me!" Logan cried. The darkness engulfed him as he sat upright. Then he heard a knock at his door.

"What?" Logan asked.

"Keep it down in there. It's four in the morning," said an irritated voice on the other side of the door.

Logan shook his head and wiped the sleep from his eyes. With his heart still pounding, he laid back down but found that sleep eluded him as his mind replayed the nightmare.

---

Connor sat at his desk, reading the instructions for the drone. The device sat on a table across from him. Sundae was lying on her bed next to Connor, listening to him complain about the directions, when the elevator chimed and Kate walked in.

"Good morning, you two. Oh, what do we have here?" Kate asked as she examined the parts strewn across the table.

"'Some assembly required,' it said," Connor replied.

"Looks more like lots of assembly required."

Kate set her things on her desk and moved her chair next to Connor's.

"How about I read the directions and you assemble?" she asked.

Kate picked up the directions and began reading step by step until her desk phone rang.

"Stroup, how may I help?"

As he listened to the one-sided conversation, Connor attached a small part that held a camera on the belly of the drone.

"And he just now discovered this?" Kate asked. "We'll head right over there." She hung up the phone.

"The Wright brothers and sisters will have to wait on taking their first flight. We have a lead to follow up on with the Sawyer case."

Connor set down the part he held in his hand, grabbed his sport coat, and put it on. Sundae was up and wagging her tail as the three of them headed for the elevator. They drove to 2341 Edwards Street. When they got out of the car, Connor and Kate had a clear side view of what was left of 2255 Decker Street.

"Why would this neighbor come forward now with this? "Connor asked as he shut the car door.

Mr. Giovanni, a short, stocky man with dark thinning hair, in his fifties, met them midway down his driveway.

"I'm Detective Maxwell. This is my partner

Detective Stroup and our canine, Sundae." Connor made the introductions.

"Detectives, I'm glad you're here. I called the police department because I was replacing two of my security cameras." Giovanni turned and pointed to one over his garage door and another by his front door. "Once I did that, I figured 'Why not replace the recorder, too?' Follow me." Giovanni led them into his three-car garage, where they found a table on which sat a recorder and monitor.

"I thought I would review the recordings before replacing everything, tapes included, when I saw IT," Giovanni said.

"And what would IT be?" asked Connor.

"Sit."

Giovanni motioned to two stools and grabbed a tape from a large stack on his shop table. He turned on the electronics.

"The day after the fire, you know the one that took poor Joel Sawyer's life, God rest his soul," Giovanni said, making the sign of the cross. "I thought I'd reviewed the security footage, but I guess I missed this."

Giovanni hit play. The darkened monitor flickered with horizontal lines of gray and black until Giovanni stopped. On the right side of the screen was an orange glow coming from the direction of the Sawyer home. Giovanni then advanced two more frames.

"There!" Giovanni thrust a short finger at the monitor, pointing toward the street that was edged by the forest. He paused the machine.

Connor squinted at the grainy image as Kate leaned forward and did the same.

"Here, let me back it up."

A dark figure dressed in black emerged from behind the Sawyer house. It stopped and watched the fire before walking toward the street. The two detectives looked at the image.

"Here, let me back it up and show you again," Giovanni said.

Connor and Kate watched closely.

"Mr. Giovanni, may we take this with us? We'd like our tech guys to try and enhance it, see if we can make out any of the person's features," Connor said.

"You can take the machine, too. The only thing I want is the monitor for my new machine…I hope this helps."

"We need only the tape. We can give you a receipt for it and return it to you once we're through with it," Connor said.

"The word around the neighborhood is this was a murder. Mr. Sawyer was such a good neighbor. May he rest in peace. Sad, very sad that someone would do this to him." Mr. Giovanni crossed himself again and wiped tears from his eyes.

---

After work, Connor met with the Natick Sheriff's Department's drone pilot in a vacant field behind the Sheriff's Department. Connor carried the Autel Robotics EVO II drone over to Pilot Graham Kenner.

"Connor Maxwell," Connor said as shook hands with Officer Kenner.

"Graham Kenner. That is one powerful drone you've got there."

"I got it online. Read reviews of different drones. I wanted something quiet that could take good images. Plus, it was on sale with free shipping.

"4k camera?" Kenner asked.

"No, it has 6k HDR video, two sonar sensors, and twelve sensing cameras. Whatever all that means," Connor said.

"Sounds great! What's the flight time?"

"Forty minutes. Anyway, that's what the paper said."

"Did Lakewood PD spring for this?"

"No, I did, but I'll put in for reimbursement. We'll see if the department will do anything. If not, I just bought myself a really expensive toy."

"Okay, I printed out the registration form for the drone, unless you already took care of this."

"I did," Connor said.

"Well, then, let's see how this bird flies!" Kenner took the remote controller from Connor and looked it over. "Nice, really nice!" he said.

---

The following night, Logan was walking down Nova Street toward the Clam Shell. As he turned the corner, an elderly man passed on his right. When Logan looked up, his mouth dropped open and his eyes widened.

"Dad, Dad?" Logan called out.

The elderly man continued walking. Logan shook his head as if to get the man's image out of his brain. Seeing a nearby bench, he hurried over and sat, his heart and head pounding.

Kate cleaned off her desk and locked up her files, her routine before leaving the office for the day. When she was ready to leave, the desk phone rang. Connor looked up.

"Go. I'll take the call for you," Connor said picking up her line. "Maxwell…you did? Hang on, we'll be right down."

Connor motioned for Kate to hold the elevator door.

"What?" Kate asked.

"They enhanced Giovanni's video. Thought you'd want to take a look," Connor said as they got on the elevator together.

CHAPTER 28

The Lakewood Police Department's basement housed its own testing lab. While it was nothing compared to the state lab or the FBI lab in Quantico, VA, their CSI team could collect material from crime scenes, run many tests, and analyze it. They did some phone traces and extracted data from phones as well as computers. A new unit followed social media, enhancing photos and videos along with several other things. Connor and Kate watched as the tech cued up Giovanni's video.

"What I did was enhance the video as much as possible," the forensic video tech said. "However, this still didn't improve the quality as much as I wanted. So, I sent it to another lab we use, which has much more sophisticated equipment. They can also testify in court if need be."

The tech pressed the fast forward on the machine and stopped, referring to his notes on a tablet.

"Okay, here." The tech froze the frame.

"We can see where a lone person walks toward the street."

He advanced to another frame, where the person turned, stood, and appeared to watch the house burn. For a few seconds, the glow of the fire danced across the person's face. The tech froze the frame on that screen.

"Looks like a male," Connor said.

"Thin-hipped, tall," Kate added.

"How about now?" the tech asked as he zoomed in on the subject.

Connor and Kate looked closely. Kate shook her head.

"The camera captured the image from across the street. I couldn't say one way or another for sure," Connor said. "It looks like a tall male dressed in dark clothes. Could it be Logan?" He turned to Kate.

"Look at the way he stands. Maybe that will help. I can print out a hard copy of this frame for your files," the tech said as he clicked the remote a few times. A laser printer in the corner printed out the image.

"Well, one thing's for sure. We know who it isn't," Kate said, smiling.

"Yep, too tall for Cole," Connor said.

"While we're down here, we should see if Logan has posted on social media since the incident at the law firm. I'll check with the tech and meet you back up at the office," Kate said.

---

The following day, Connor, Kate, and Sundae met Graham Kenner at Abe Harley's ranch. The sun had barely poked its lazy head over the mountains.

The night before, Connor had made sure all the batteries were charged and the drone was ready for flight. He had asked Graham to pilot the drone over the ranch. Still feeling like a novice, he didn't want to botch the operation, and Graham was only too eager to volunteer to fly this new drone. Sundae sniffed at the drone as it was placed on the ground. Graham reached out and pet Sundae.

"This could put you out of a job," he told her as she wagged her tail.

"Unless that thing can track by scent, I don't think she has anything to worry about," Connor said.

"That's true. Let's get this bird in the air!" Graham said. The drone took flight.

Graham remarked on how easy the drone was to fly as he showed Connor how he was doing things.

Kate and Sundae stood watching the men.

"They look more like two little boys with a new toy than two law enforcement agents, don't they?" Kate asked as she pet Sundae's soft ears while sipping on a latte.

---

The flight over the ranch yielded nothing with regard to Logan's disappearance. Connor, Kate, and Sundae returned to the police department for their meeting with Beth Ellis. When they arrived, Detectives Barton and Harris were already in the conference room with Beth.

"You're late," Bob said jokingly, tapping the face of his watch. Grant and Beth laughed.

"How'd the drone flight go?" asked Grant.

"Nothing. Saw a lot of guys in uniforms but no Logan or his car." Connor sounded disheartened.

"Well, I have the reason for that," Beth said as she pulled a file from her bag. "I got the report back from the CAST unit."

Beth handed each of the detectives a copy of the report.

"As you can see, Logan is no longer in the state. Or, at least, his phone isn't. He's in Florida.

"Florida?" Kate asked.

"Turn the page. Note the aerial shot in your report. Seems he spends most of his time here."

"It looks a lot like the ranch we just came from. Look at the buildings and layout," Connor said, looking at Kate.

"Our people at Quantico have this group on their radar. They call themselves the Brotherhood. They're an extremist group. The bureau is trying to find out where they're getting the funds to buy up all this land and build on it. They started in the southeast part of the United States and are making their way across the US," Beth said.

"Follow the money trail," Bob said.

"Logan is part of this group?" Kate asked.

"It appears so," Beth said. "They recruit people at a young age."

Connor wrote the information on a legal pad.

"So, can we assume this group here in the southwest is part of the same group in Florida?" Connor asked.

"More than likely," Beth answered. "We have an agent working inside the group to gain more information. I've requested that they let me know if they find out anything. I'll let them know about the group here as well and see if they can get some intel on Logan," Beth said.

"These date stamps on the reports…can I assume they're the dates when Logan has been in Florida?" Connor asked.

"Yes, my guy at the bureau mentioned he frequents a bar called the Clam Shell. If you look at the last page, you'll see the address," Beth answered.

Maggie parked in the visitor lot and turned off the engine. Cole had been back at school for only five days. As she waited for Cole, Maggie picked up her magazine and scanned a few pages, glancing at her watch every few minutes. After thirty minutes had passed, she became worried. The stream of departing students had dwindled to just a few stragglers. Where was he? She looked around. After glancing at her watch again, Maggie decided to go inside and check. She went to the information desk, where she found a young woman in her twenties.

"Hello. I was supposed to pick up a student this afternoon, Cole...Cole Sawyer. He never came out."

Maggie waited but the young woman didn't respond.

"Can someone check his last class and see if maybe he's still there...or something?" Maggie asked, distress creeping into her voice.

"Take a seat. I'll call security," the young woman said as she picked up the desk phone. She looked out over the desk and called out to Maggie. "What was his name again?"

Maggie sighed heavily. "Cole Sawyer."

"I'll hold," the young woman said to someone on the other end of the line.

Several minutes passed.

"I'll tell her, thank you."

Maggie was already up from her seat. "Tell me what?" Maggie demanded.

The young woman replaced the phone and conveyed the message that security had given her. "Cole didn't show up to his last three classes."

Overcome with worry, Maggie started to shake.

She began digging through her purse, looking for Kate's card, but couldn't find it.

"Call the Lakewood Police Department," Maggie demanded.

"Ma'am, your son probably just…"

"Oh my God. Call your security person. I'll talk to them! Please, call the Lakewood Police." Maggie barked the order.

"Why do we need the police? Your son probably just ditched his last three classes, that's all," protested the young woman.

Maggie reached over the desk and grabbed the woman's hand. "Call your security person, NOW! And he is not my son."

CHAPTER 29

The Lakewood dispatcher transferred the call to Kate's cell phone. Meanwhile, the police department had already dispatched a patrolman to the school.

"Stroup," Kate answered the call.

The hysterical voice of Maggie Ortega—half-talking, half-crying—came across the phone. "Kate, he's gone! I came to pick him up and Cole's gone."

"Slow down, Maggie." Kate tried to calm her but to no avail.

"The school said he missed his last three classes. Cole can't drive…and he would never try to walk home from this distance. Kate, something is wrong, very wrong. You have to come quick!"

"Maggie, where are you now?" Kate asked.

"I'm still at the school. They're sending an officer out. Please come quick. What if Logan took him?" Maggie cried.

"I'm on my way."

Kate disconnected the call and turned to Connor.

"Turn around. That was Maggie. We need to go to Cole's school. He's missing. He missed his last three classes and no one has seen him."

"Better have Maggie call his attorney so he can notify the DA. He was out on bail only until the trial or until we could prove someone else killed his dad and Mr. Potts." Connor swung around the car. "Ask Sandy to put out a BOLO for Cole. Call Beth and ask her if CAST can see where Logan has been for the last few hours."

Connor maneuvered through traffic, dodging cars, traffic lights, and slow-moving vehicles. He moved slightly into the oncoming car lane to leave room for a man changing a flat tire on the side of the road,

"God, this is going to look bad for Cole, like he jumped bail and fled," Kate said as she called Sandy.

Connor pulled the car to a stop in the parking

lot next to the marked patrol car. He, Kate, and Sundae dashed into the building.

"Kate!" Maggie yelled and ran to her. Connor went directly to the uniformed officer, who was holding a black backpack.

"I found this." The officer held up the backpack.

Connor reached into his jacket pocket, pulled out a pair of gloves, and put them on before taking the backpack from the patrolman. He opened one compartment of the backpack and found Cole's cell phone, which Connor assumed that Cole used to text instead of call. Scrolling, he saw several unanswered messages from Maggie. The rest of the backpack contained papers, pens, pencils, and school books. Inside the back flap, behind a plastic stitched holder, Connor found a photo of Cole and Joel.

Turning to the patrolman, Connor said, "Show me where you found the backpack."

The patrolman walked outside the building. Connor and Sundae followed him into the parking lot, then beyond the fence. About fifty yards farther, the patrolman pointed.

"There. It looked like it was just tossed there."

Connor opened the backpack and held it to Sundae's nose. "Find Cole."

The thirteen-inch beagle sniffed the ground and

traveled in a zig-zag motion across the field. Connor and the patrolman followed. Sundae went out into a field dotted with brush.

She sat abruptly and barked. Connor went to her side as she howled in front of a man's blue coat.

"Release," Connor commanded.

Sundae stopped howling. Still wearing his gloves, Connor bent down and examined the size-medium coat. Picking it up, he saw blood around the neck and right sleeve.

"Do me a favor. Get Detective Stroup and ask her to bring a crime scene bag for this. Tell her we need a DNA sample of the blood on this coat. Also, ask Sandy to dispatch the CSI team to this locale. If you haven't already gotten a statement from Maggie, get it now," Connor said to the patrolman. He then laid the backpack down and began looking around.

"Sundae, find Cole," Connor commanded.

She began her zig-zag searching pattern of the area once more. Kate came over, put on her gloves, and bagged the coat. When she noticed the blood, she was glad the patrolman had detained Maggie for a report. Kate placed a marker so that the CSI team would know where the jacket had been discovered. She could hear Connor and Sundae off in the distance but decided to return to Maggie.

Sundac sniffed around the brush and trees, then out to a road behind the school. She stopped at a gravel patch next to the road and howled. Connor gave the release command. All he could see was gravel that had marks, presumably made by shoes. Connor guessed someone had dragged Cole in this area and, most likely, forced him into a car to transport him. It was obvious that there had been a struggle, as Connor saw bloodstains in the gravel.

He looked out at the road, which he presumed led to the back of the school for deliveries. Nonetheless, he and Sundae walked to the end of the pavement to make sure Cole wasn't there. Sundae ran ahead, stopped, and howled again. Connor released her and bent down to find the ankle monitor that the court had issued to Cole. Or, at least, he assumed it was Coles'. Cole, or someone else, had cut the bracelet off his ankle, most likely so that Cole could not be traced. Either way, Connor knew this would not look good to the DA's office. When he picked up the monitor, he saw blood on the strap.

Connor had stalled the DA until the rapid DNA test had come back. It was positive proof that the blood found on Cole's coat was, in fact, his own. Still, Connor had the CSI team send it off to the crime lab, as he knew that rapid testing could not be used in court. The RDNA test was simply a tool that law enforcement used until the crime lab get them a test that could be used as evidence if necessary. The next step was a meeting with the DA, which Connor knew could go either way. With the results in hand, he and Kate headed over to One Plaza to meet with the DA, Cole's attorney, Judd Dale, Maggie Ortega, and Beth Ellis.

Without saying a word, the DA looked over the offense incident report taken when Cole presumably was abducted from his school. Next, she picked up the rapid DNA report, then reviewed the photos taken at the crime scene. Lastly was Beth Ellis' report, showing the whereabouts of Logan's cell phone. She set all the paperwork on her desk with a heavy sigh and then looked up at the group of people sitting in front of her desk. The DA cleared her throat.

CHAPTER 30

"I don't need to tell you how this looks to the courts," the DA said, gazing sternly at the group sitting on the other side of her desk.

"I can assure you; Cole would never leave on his own," said Maggie, fighting back tears. "The boy has never learned to drive. He doesn't have friends like other young men his age, go to parties, or even drink. His professors are the only ones Cole can really relate to. Someone has taken him! We need to find him."

"Ms. Ortega, Mr. Sawyer is not on trial for DWI. This is a murder case. It doesn't matter whether he drinks, goes to parties, or drives. What matters is that he is suspected of killing his adopted father, Joel Sawyer and his friend, Fletcher Potts.

"I'm sorry. I just know in my heart…" Maggie stopped talking as Kate touched her arm.

"Officer Maxwell, did the DNA found on the ankle monitor belong to Cole?" the DA asked.

"It was, in fact, Cole's. We did find someone else's, too, but there isn't a match in our local database, nor the COTIS," Connor explained.

"In light of the other information that Ms. Ellis presented, knowing the charges and reports of a pending arrest of the older son, Logan Sawyer, I will give you forty-eight hours to find Cole…and the answers to what happened. I've already talked to the judge about this. Am I clear?' the DA asked.

Maggie started to open her mouth but Kate shook her head no.

---

Cole woke up to a piercing pain over his right temple, a pounding headache, and blurry vision. When his sight cleared, he looked around. He was locked in some type of metal cage inside a building, maybe a warehouse or basement. A single light hung from the ceiling. He turned his line of sight away from the light. The brightness hurt his eyes.

He couldn't remember anything beyond walking

to class that morning. The next thing he knew, he was here, wherever this place was. Unable to yell for help, he pulled himself off the cot, stood on wobbly legs, and shook the cage. The bottom, sides, and top were constructed of thick-gauge wire. He tried to bend it, but the wire wouldn't move. Inside the cage were a bucket, two blankets, a pillow, a cot, and some water bottles. Why was he here and, more so, how did he get here? In one way, it reminded him of when he had been put in jail last month and Detective Maxwell and his dog, Sundae, had stayed with him. But this was really nothing like that. It was more like an animal cage.

Cole's mathematical mind began to analyze the cage. Approximately twelve feet in length, seven feet tall, eight feet wide. He quickly came up with ninety-six square feet of floor space, but not why he was here. Where was his backpack, with his books, pens, and notebook? How would he communicate with people if he didn't have a pen and his notebook? Cole lay back down on the cot and, feeling a chill in the air, pulled the blankets over him. He'd been wearing a coat that morning when he left Maggie's house but now it, too, was gone.

He couldn't see any windows but at least he still had his watch. He was hungry. He couldn't remember having lunch today and it was now dinnertime. Or, it would've been at Maggie's house. He imagined Maggie's cozy kitchen and the delicious aroma of food wafting through the air as she cooked. God, how he wished he were there as he drifted off to sleep.

---

"This is Candy Martin of the Channel Seven News."

With the backdrop of One City Plaza behind her and the news van to her right, Candy continued. "We've just learned of a surprising new development in the double homicide case of the two elderly men who were shot and their bodies burned in their Lakewood home. Today, the suspect who has been charged with the double homicide and was released on bond with an ankle bracelet has disappeared. The bracelet and some of his belongings were found outside the school he attended."

The station inserted a photo of Cole Sawyer.

Candy Martin's voice-over could be heard saying, "If you've seen this man, please call the Lakewood Police Department at the number shown below the photo. Be advised that the man is unable to speak."

The station segued to the next news story. Connor turned off the living room TV. He sat, wondering who had leaked the story to the news media. They were supposed to have forty-eight hours to bring in Logan and look for Cole. He pondered where Cole could be. From Beth, he knew that the bureau's CAST unit could see that Logan, or at least his phone, was still in Florida. They had given the information on Logan to the Florida State Troopers and asked them to pick him up.

Connor grabbed his truck keys. At the sound of metal jingling, Sundae bounced out of her bed. She looked at Connor to see if she would get to go with him.

"Let's practice flying the drone," Connor said, walking out to the garage.

Sundae followed, wagging her tail with approval. She knew that going in the truck meant going for a ride or hiking. Connor reached for the drone on his workbench, then carefully set it in the back seat before opening the passenger-side door for Sundae.

With it being his day off, Connor drove to a mesa and found a good place to park. He took his backpack with extra batteries, along with water for himself and Sundae, and had the drone flying within a few minutes. Sundae tilted her head from side to side as if attempting to figure out what this thing was. Connor bent down with the controller and showed the display panel to Sundae. However, the little beagle was unimpressed and walked away.

"You'll see. Some day this will make our job easier." Connor laughed, remembering what the Natick Sheriff's Department pilot had told Sundae — that someday it would put her out of a job.

Connor had told everyone that he was out honing his drone flying skills. Nonetheless, he was also was aware that he was still looking for Mia Gordon's body. Mia was a young woman who had been abducted years ago. The man who took her, Jared Allen Hobbs, had been caught and sent to prison, where he hanged himself. Unfortunately, he took the whereabouts of Mia's body to the grave. Connor had spent his days off hiking the hills and mountains around Lakewood, looking for her body. He was a detective who simply never gave up. Connor thought the drone might give him an edge in finding Mia and finally giving closure to her father.

Connor knew the dumping sites that Hobbs had used for his kills. Hobbs never took the time to bury his victims. He simply dumped the bodies unclothed in remote areas. With the amount of time that had passed since Mia's disappearance, Connor knew that the only thing left would be dried bones. More than likely, those would have been scattered around by wildlife.

After three hours of finding nothing, Connor loaded up his gear and Sundae and headed home. Kate had invited him to join her for dinner, which he was looking forward to. Checking his watch, he saw that he had enough time to shower, shave, and feed Sundae before going over to the Lakota.

Kate was already seated when Connor walked in. She stood and waved him to their table. If someone asked her what it was about the way Connor walked, she would never in a million years be able to put it in words. He walked with confidence but there was something else that was just so sexy about him. He was wearing a tan sport coat, a light tan button-down shirt with a blue pinstripe, Wrangler jeans, and, as always, his western boots.

"Come here often, Cowboy?" Kate asked with a big smile.

Connor smiled and took a seat. "Been waiting long?"

"No, they just brought me to our table. I did order you a water with lemon."

"Thanks," Connor said as the waiter placed a glass on the table.

"Do you two need some time to look over the menu?" the waitress asked.

"Yes, please," Kate answered.

Connor perused the menu, then set it aside after deciding on an entrée.

"So, how did your piloting go?"

"Fine, but I was thinking you should learn how to fly it, too," Connor replied.

"Me? Why?"

"Remember when I took off up the mountain after Cole? You could've gone back, grabbed the drone, and kept an eye on what was going on, maybe even guided me to Cole."

CHAPTER 31

Connor didn't want the evening with Kate to end. She was so easy to talk to and she genuinely listened, not pretending or simply nodding. He knew that some women would be bored, but Kate was different. He wondered if it was because they had so much in common, including their job. Could it be that Kate was just gifted in communication skills? She certainly had a gift for calming people, gently breaking bad news to the families of loved ones. The woman was beautiful and elegant and she understood men. Connor thought this was because she worked with mostly men.

He walked Kate to her car and thanked her for the evening. As they looked at each other, Connor leaned in and could smell the soft, sweet scent of her perfume and hair. He held her for a minute, then kissed her. What was starting to be a long, lingering kiss was interrupted by a text to both of them. It was Connor who pulled away first and looked at his phone. The text was from Bob Barton and it was short and to the point. Logan had been picked up and was being held in Florida. Advise.

---

Connor and Kate returned to the station.

"I'll go pick up Logan. It's been a while since I've been to redneck Hawaii," Bob said as he picked up the phone to call his wife and let her know. Kate booked the first flight from Lakewood to Daytona Beach. It was a red-eye to Florida that night and would get Bob to the Daytona airport in the early morning.

---

Connor and Kate locked up the file cabinets. As they were about to head for the elevator, the desk phone rang.

"Connor, can you come to the booking room?

I'm not sure what's going on but I can see a prisoner on the floor and a patrolman fighting with him," the dispatcher said.

"Be right there," Connor said.

"What is it?" Kate asked, trying to catch up with Connor. She jumped into the elevator with him.

"Not sure. The dispatcher said she was watching the camera in the booking room when a fight broke out," Connor said, pushing the elevator button several times.

Once on the first floor, Connor and Kate quickly handed their guns to the dispatcher to lock up in the desk drawer before running to the booking room. A young Hispanic male was handcuffed, lying on his stomach on the floor. A patrolman was kicking the young man, then got down and kidney punched him.

"ENOUGH!" Connor roared at the officer, pulling him off the man.

"Who the...hell do you think you are?" the patrolman demanded.

"Detective Connor Maxwell," Connor answered. "Kate, check on the prisoner."

Connor pulled the patrolman out of the room and into the hallway.

"You can't do this!" yelled the patrolman, his face red with anger and his fists clenched.

"I just did! Who is your sergeant?" Connor asked.

"Screw you," Patrolman Torino spat the words as Connor held him against the wall.

"I asked you a question, patrolman," Connor repeated. The patrolman struggled, trying to pull away from Connor.

Back in the booking room, Kate gently turned the man over. He was bleeding from the mouth and coughing up blood.

"Why were you arrested?" Kate asked.

"He said," the man coughed several times, "he said I was going fifteen miles over the speed limit."

"But that's a ticket. Why were you brought in here?"

"He told me I wasn't…" The young man trailed off and lost consciousness.

Kate ran out of the room and toward the dispatcher. She requested that an ambulance be dispatched to the PD.

When Connor saw an EMT pushing a gurney down the hallway, he pointed to the booking room and prevented the patrolman from going back in.

"We can take over from here," said the EMT.

Kate got up from the floor, stepped aside, and went out into the hallway with Connor.

"Kate, find out from dispatch who Patrolman Torino's sergeant is and request that he come in ASAP," Connor said.

When Kate had returned, Connor turned to the patrolman.

"What was the arrest for?" he asked.

"Look, I don't have to answer to you or your little girlfriend," Torino said.

"He pulled over the guy for going fifteen miles over the speed limit, then started to search his car," explained Kate. "The kid asked why. He said that the next thing he knew, the patrolman was tossing him on the hood of his car."

With that, Connor pulled the bodycam off the patrolman's chest and handed it over to Kate.

"Give this to the dispatcher. Tell her to save the recording of the booking room, too."

After the dispatcher gave him a quick briefing, Sergeant Mike Baca walked back to where Connor held the patrolman.

"I'll take it from here, detectives. I'll need a statement from both of you by tomorrow," the sergeant said as the EMTs rolled out the young man.

The EMT asked the officers, "Do you need him cuffed to the rails?"

"For now, yes, until I can view the body cam and get all the details." the sergeant replied.

The sergeant took the patrolman to his office, while Connor and Kate walked to the dispatch desk to retrieve their guns.

"There's nothing I hate worse than a bad cop. That kid wasn't a threat to him, none whatsoever. It's cops like him who give us all a bad name. The kid was cuffed…" Connor said, shaking his head.

"What do you think will happen to Torino?" Kate asked.

"After Internal Affairs and the city's legal eagles finish with him, he'll be lucky to be riding a Segway as a mall cop."

---

The following day, Bob picked up Logan from the jail in Daytona and escorted him back to Lakewood on charges of attempted murder of Attorney John Sheldon, great bodily injury, eluding a police officer, and property damage over one thousand dollars. While they believed Logan had the strongest motive, and he was at the top of the police department's suspect list, they couldn't charge him for the murder of his father or the possible disappearance of his adopted brother, Cole. However, at least they'd be able to hold and question him. As soon as the plane touched down, they would bring Logan to the box for questioning.

CHAPTER 32

Kate questioned Logan, as he seemed to be more responsive to her than to Connor.

"Logan, just tell me where Cole is. I can talk to the DA and get some of the charges reduced or maybe even dropped," Kate said.

"I told you already. I have no idea where he is." There was a long period of silence. "My guess is, he got scared and took off."

Kate waited a few minutes.

"Did you have someone from the Brotherhood pick up Cole?"

"No. Why would I do that? The kid is guilty. I told you that. It's only a matter of time before he's in jail. Did his lady friend lose her little house because of the brat?"

Kate knew Logan was referring to Maggie's house, which she had put up for Cole's bail. She noted that he didn't deny or confirm his alliance with the Brotherhood.

"No, but she probably will if we can't find him."

Connor was already losing his patience with Logan as he stood in the hallway, watching and listening to the interview through the one-way glass. He had no clue how Kate could stand talking to Logan. He was a privileged guy who'd never had to work for anything in his life. The fact that a woman could lose her home, which she had worked hard for, meant nothing to him.

"Good!" Logan tipped his chair back from the metal table as far as his cuffed hands would allow.

"Logan, the police in Florida said they talked to a guy you were with on the night they picked you up."

"Yeah? Is it a crime to talk to someone in a bar?" Logan asked.

"No, it's not, but he told authorities that you mentioned you had something you might want taken care of…some unfinished business."

Kate could see this caught Logan off guard. She

knew he had no idea the police had talked to the guy who had been sitting beside him at the Clam Shell.

"Look, the guy is lying. I was having a drink there, that's all."

"The bartender said that on several occasions you and Mr. Chaney met there to talk. Mr. Chaney said the same thing."

Logan smiled and shook his head. Kate closed her notebook and stood. Logan sat up.

"So, you're not going to help me get out of here, right?" Logan asked. Kate sat down and looked Logan straight in the eye.

"No, not unless you help me find Cole. Then I'd be happy to. Now, if you'll excuse me, I have other things to do."

"I didn't kill my father and his friend. I just want what is mine by birthright. Cole isn't my brother. He shouldn't have anything left by my father. I'm his biological son, not Cole."

"Is that why you attacked Attorney Sheldon?"

"I just wanted what was mine. He said no, that he was following my father's wishes."

"The attorney can't give you anything. You're still a suspect in your father's murder."

"The police picked up Cole for that crime."

"I think you know why the DA had the police pick up Cole. It was a tip you called in. You tried to sell that story to Detective Maxwell and me. When we didn't buy it, you called it into the DA's office."

Logan didn't respond. Kate got up and exited the room.

---

As near as Cole could tell, he'd spent the night in this cage. A person had brought in a meal for breakfast and one for lunch. It was now dinnertime again and his stomach was growling. If this was jail, why weren't Detectives Maxwell and Stroup here? Where were Sundae, Maggie, and his attorney? Last night, before he fell asleep, he realized that the ankle bracelet was gone. He'd been told that could be removed only by the bail bondsman or the courts. So, if this wasn't jail, what was it and why was he being held here?

---

Connor, Kate, and Sundae went back to Cole's school and asked to view any footage from the exterior cameras. The school's security guard allowed them to watch the footage. At around ten o'clock on the morning Cole disappeared, a heavy, dark cloth of some type was placed on camera number five, which looked out over the school parking lot. All they had to go on was a timeline that Cole had been abducted shortly after ten in the morning or had left on his own. Connor had to ask himself how Cole could have left on his own. He had no money other than the few dollars Maggie had given him for emergencies. He couldn't drive and had no real friends except for his professors.

"Maybe we should talk to his professors in the morning," Connor said. "They might have seen something or know something."

"I'll go ask at the front desk."

Kate walked to the information desk.

"Excuse me," she said. "Is there any way Detective Maxwell and I can speak to Cole's professors, either today or tomorrow?"

The young lady looked up from her computer screen as if Kate had interrupted a very important assignment that she was working on for the school. However, from the angle where she was standing, Kate could see a social media page on the computer screen. Brushing a lock of purple hair from her forehead, the woman thought for a minute.

"I'll have to ask the dean," she said in a high, shrill voice that made the hair on the back of Kate's neck stand up.

"And...can you do that?"

Without saying a word, the woman pushed away from the desk and wobbled away on stacked heeled shoes. After some time had passed, Kate was about to leave and go back to Connor when the girl wobbled back, plopped down on her desk chair, pushed the same lock of purple hair from her forehead, and looked up.

"I spoke to Dean Hillson. He's contacting Mr. Sawyer's professors. It seems that all but one professor has agreed."

"May I ask why the one didn't want to talk to us?"

"Oh, he was out sick yesterday and today. The dean didn't want to bother him at home. The dean said he'll have you meet with him and the professors at ten tomorrow in his office."

With that, the young woman returned to her screen.

"Thank you," Kate said.

When the young woman didn't acknowledge her or look up, Kate walked back to Connor, who was still looking through the security tapes.

"We can meet tomorrow with all but one of Coles' professors at ten o'clock in the dean's office."

"What's with the one who can't meet with us?" Connor asked.

"Out sick. Maybe he'll be back tomorrow," Kate said. "Did you find anything we missed on the tapes?"

"No," Connor said, pushing away from the desk and rubbing his bloodshot eyes.

The following day, Connor and Kate met with all of Cole's professors in the dean's office. Even the one who had called in sick managed to show up. All seem genuinely concerned that a student may have been taken from the school. The dean said that security had been beefed up to protect students and staff. The one thing every professor agreed on was that while Cole was extremely smart, he did not have the ability to leave on his own.

Connor, Kate, and Sundae left the dean's office. As they passed through the double doors, a student stopped in front of them. Connor and Kate moved to the side.

"Are you the police?" asked a ninety-pound girl haphazardly carrying what Connor thought looked like a hundred and fifty pounds of books.

The three stopped and the girl bent down to

stroke Sundae's long, soft ears. The student had blue eyes and her face was framed by bright orange hair that resembled a Brillo pad.

"Detectives Maxwell and Stroup. Is anything wrong?" Connor asked, looking beyond the girl.

"No," the girl said, setting her books on a bench.

"And your name is?" Kate asked.

"Claire. Claire Jennings."

"Claire, is there something we can do for you?" asked Connor.

"I heard about Cole and the day he went missing. Well, I saw something odd."

CHAPTER 33

Kate put her arm around Claire's shoulder. Instinctively, she knew that the girl was upset. Kate saw a bench and motioned toward it. They sat on the old iron bench in a xeriscape area beside the door. The girl appeared to study the plants as a lazy lizard sunbathed on a decorative rock.

"What do you mean by odd?" Kate asked.

Connor bent down next to Sundae, watching Claire.

"It was the day Cole went missing. We always pass each other. He's coming from the outer building." She pointed toward a greenish metal building outside the main campus area. "I'm going toward it for my next class. I always say hi to him, as he can hear just fine. He just can't speak, as I'm sure you know. He made me a page in his notebook that said 'Hi, Claire.' He would always have the page ready and hold it up for me and smile.

Last week, I showed him an app I found on the app store that he could download. It's called 'Talk for Me' or something like that. I can't remember now. With the app, he can type in words and his phone talks for him. He created a 'Hi, Claire, how are you?' and started to use it just for me. So, the other day when we passed, there was no page in the notebook or phone talking for him. I said hi and got nothing. No smile. Nothing."

"Claire, maybe he was in a hurry or didn't see you," Kate said.

"I would agree but he looked right at me. He had a man on each side of him, and he looked really scared. I said, 'Hi, Cole' for the second time. The men seemed in a hurry to get him out of the parking lot."

"Why didn't you say something to a professor, school security, or the dean?" Connor asked.

"I was going to talk to my professor but after watching the men and Cole, I was late to class. I tried once in the classroom and the professor said that whatever it was, it could wait until after class. Then I forgot. When they sent out the newsletter today about Cole and said that they were bringing in extra security for us students and the staff, I got worried. I just talked to the lady at the desk and she pointed toward you two."

"Can you tell me what the two men looked like?" Connor asked.

Claire's hands were in her lap and she was nervously picking at some loose skin around a fingernail.

"They both wore dark suits. Blue, I think, or maybe black." Claire pushed up her glasses.

Kate opened her notebook and began writing down what Claire was saying.

"Before I got close to them, the two men were talking. They weren't speaking English."

"Do you have any idea what language they were speaking?" Kate asked.

"I have no idea. I assume Cole knew. He's fluent in several languages."

"Did you see where the two men took Cole?"

"I turned and watched them but one of my professors came out of the building and told me I should get along to my class."

"After school, do you think you could come into

the Lakewood Police Department and sit down with our sketch artist?" Connor asked.

"I can try but I had only a few seconds to look at them."

"Claire, this may help us find Cole," Kate said.

"I could come over around six o'clock. Would that be okay?"

"That would be fine. We probably won't be there. Give your name at the front desk and tell the person that you're supposed to meet with the police department's sketch artist. They'll call him."

---

Connor got home while there was still daylight. He had been home for a little over an hour when he noticed a drawing of Sundae that he'd been working on. He walked over and flipped on the overhead lamp clamped to the drawing table. Sitting down, he picked up a 3H drawing pencil and began to add shading. He loved to draw but mostly his art consisted of pencil sketches of Sundae or mechanical things. He told his friends that drawing was like therapy and helped him relax.

Soon the house was completely dark except for the lamp over his small drawing table. The ringing of his phone pulled Connor out of the zone, as he called it.

"Maxwell."

"Detective, Harper Huckabee."

Harper had worked for the Lakewood Police Department for about six years. He'd once had dreams of being a famous artist, with his work displayed on the walls of museums and in gallery exhibits. After two years of being a starving artist, Harper had seen an ad in the paper for a sketch artist for the Lakewood PD. After applying and interviewing with the department, he landed the job.

Harper's sketches were so realistic, they looked like they should be hanging on a wall, not appearing on the six o'clock news. The previous Lakewood sketch artist did simple black and white pencil sketches. Connor used to say they looked more like stick people. Harper added so much more detail. Once he decided to add color to his sketches, he requested an electronic tablet. The police department purchased a tablet that, when connected to his computer, took his sketches to the next level.

"What have you got, Harper?" Connor asked.

"Claire came in. I should have the sketches to

you by tomorrow. From what she described; the two men look to be Asian."

After Connor disconnected the call, he sat there thinking. Asian? Claire had said they were talking in another language. What the hell was going on? He slid his desk chair to a file cabinet and pulled out the photos that the drone had taken of the Brotherhood. There were no Asian-looking men there. He looked at his watch.

"Sundae, you're slipping. It's way past dinnertime!"

Connor's words woke up Sundae. She stood, shook her ears, and began wagging her tail. She knew what dinnertime meant. Connor quickly fed her. Next, he made himself a scrambled egg sandwich with ketchup and pickles. As he ate, he thought about Harper's call. Then he picked up his phone and called Beth.

"You still working with hypnosis?" Connor asked.

"Well, good evening to you, too. Are you having trouble sleeping and need me to…?"

Connor's laughter interrupted Beth before she could finish her sentence.

"No. We met a girl at Cole's school today who

saw two men taking Cole from the school the day he went missing."

"What's that got to do with hypnosis?"

"The girl talked to Kate and me. She said that two men speaking in another language were taking Cole from school. Cole seemed scared. Anyway, that's what she said. I had her meet with our sketch artist this evening. He just called and told me that what she was describing to him sounded like Asian men. So, I was wondering if you could work your hocus-pocus magic with hypnosis. Maybe see if you could get her to give us a few words that we could narrow down and anything else she may recall."

There was a period of silence.

"Beth, you still there?" Connor asked.

"Yes. I'm just wondering how all this fits into this case with the two murders, a house fire, and Cole. You know, Asian?"

"Beth, can you?"

Another period of silence.

"Will you do it?"

CHAPTER 34

Connor glanced at the photos on the wall behind Beth's desk. He walked around to get a closer look. They were all images from Beth's days as a profiler with the FBI, before she decided to hang her own shingle as a consultant for police departments around the US. There were even two photos of her with past presidents. Connor noticed that Beth smiled in all the photos but didn't really look happy—not like she did since she left the bureau.

Beth opened the door and entered from another room of the office.

"Oh, my wall of shame," she said. "My business manager thinks they're a great asset for my business, so I had them hung up."

"Impressive, I have to say," Connor said.

They both turned as Claire stepped into the office.

"Am I late?" Claire asked.

Connor glanced at his watch. "No, not at all. Beth, this is Claire Jennings. Claire, this is Beth Ellis."

"Claire, please have a seat. I want to start by explaining what hypnosis is not."

Claire sat. Connor and Beth also took their seats.

Beth continued. "Many people think that you're put <u>under</u> the state of hypnosis. Nothing could be further from the truth. You are not under anyone's control. I like to call it the myth of hypnosis brought about by the many fictional movies and books. Unfortunately, many of these depictions are very scary and unfounded. To date, law enforcement is using hypnosis, but many therapists are also using hypnosis to help with things like PTSD and addictive behavior, to name just a few.

"What I feel most comfortable telling people I work with is that hypnosis is, in its simplest form, a deep state of relaxation. In the case of law enforcement, this allows a person to tap into their subconscious mind, as if they were actually there at the scene. However, when hypnosis is done correctly, the subject is instructed that they are watching this as if they were sitting in the safety of their own living room or under a shade tree in their backyard. Anywhere they feel comfortable. They become an observer watching what happened.

"For the first step, I will guide you to a state of relaxation, then bring you back right away. In my experience, I have found this is best. Once people understand that they can come back, they are more likely to relax. Do you have any questions?"

"So, if I'm not in control of my body and mind, will I remember what I said?"

Connor noticed that Claire was nervously picking at her fingers.

"You have full control of your body," Beth said. "Some people remember every detail, while others can't remember anything at all. But a good hypnotherapist for law enforcement will never suggest anything. For instance, I would never say 'The car was red' or 'The lady was thin and tall.' I ask you to tell me what color you see or what the person looks like or what they are doing."

"I saw a segment on TV where a doctor did something like this," Claire replied.

"So, how do you feel about it?" Beth asked.

"I think it's worth a try if it will help Cole."

"Why don't we step into the other room and begin?"

Beth stood and opened the door. Connor followed the women into the room. Claire stopped, looking around.

"Where do you want me?" she asked as she glanced at the room.

There was an overstuffed chair, a loveseat, and a couch. To Connor, the space resembled a comfortable living room in just about any home, minus a television. The walls were painted a soft shade of blue. One wall held a photo of the ocean in soft colors and shades of blue and green that seemed as if it had been taken just for this room.

"Anywhere you'd like. Wherever you feel comfortable."

Claire tried the loveseat first, then got up and went to the overstuffed chair. It reminded Connor of the children's story "Goldilocks and the Three Bears." He could almost hear his mother's voice as she read it to him long ago: "This one was too big and this one was just right."

"Comfy?" Beth asked.

Beth and Connor watched as Claire moved

around, then leaned back as if she were testing the chair before buying it.

"Yes, very," Claire said, setting her purse on the floor.

Beth reached over and pulled a plush pale blue fleece throw from the back of the couch. She handed it to Claire. "You may get chilly. Many people do."

Claire was hesitant to take it. Beth intuitively understood.

"I wash it after each client. I wouldn't want something that had been on another person, either," Beth said as Claire took the throw.

Connor wondered how Beth could understand Claire in such a short time. He sat on the couch while Beth took a place on the loveseat across from Claire. Once Claire was comfortable, Beth started the session.

"Claire, I'd like you to close your eyes and take a deep breath in through your nose. Then let it out very slowly through your mouth." Claire closed her eyes and did as instructed.

"Good. Now this time, breathe out more slowly through your mouth."

Connor looked at Beth, then back at Claire.

Beth had her do the breathing exercise three

times. Next, she asked Claire to find a comfortable place where she liked to be and just relax. After a few minutes, Beth spoke.

"Claire, where are you?"

"I'm on the beach. The sand is so warm. I love the way it feels between my toes."

Looking at Beth, Connor raised his eyebrows, then noticed that he could see Claire's toes wiggling in her shoes. Beth allowed Claire to linger on the beach within her mind for another five minutes. Then she told Claire that she would count to ten and, on ten, that Claire would be awake and alert. Slowly, Beth counted to ten. Claire opened her eyes and looked around the room.

"Welcome back. Did you enjoy being at the beach?" Beth smiled.

"Oh, I loved it there…Wait, what? You were there?" Claire asked, puzzled.

"No, you told us. Now I'd like to do this again. Only this time, I'll be recording it for the Lakewood Police Department and I'll be asking you more questions. Remember, you're safe wherever you are. You'll just be an observer and nothing can hurt you. Any questions?"

"No," Claire answered.

"Take three deep breaths through your nose,

slowly let them out through your mouth, and go to your safe place."

Beth watched as Claire slowly relaxed.

"Claire, I'd like to ask you if you could go back to that day when you saw Cole coming toward you. Nod your head when you see him."

Claire nodded.

"Do you see him?"

Claire's face beamed with a smile.

"Now look around. Is anyone with him?"

Claire turned her head and looked.

"Yes, there are two men. I don't know who they are but as we get closer, I can see that Cole is scared."

"How do you know?" Beth asked.

"His expression. Oh, no!"

"What is it, Claire?"

"They have him by the elbows. I said hi to him and he pulled to one side. I can see they're escorting him and he's scared."

"Remember, Claire, you're safe. You're only observing what is happening," Beth said in a calm, reassuring voice.

"He's doing something with both hands. They're upset with him now," Claire said with urgency.

Connor looked over at Beth and mouthed the words "What is Cole doing?"

"Claire, go back. What is Cole doing with his hands?"

"I don't know." She furrowed her brow.

"Describe it to me or show me with your hands."

"He has one hand in a fist with his thumb sticking upward." She was silent, then spoke again. "His other hand is palm up under the hand with the fist. Wait! He's pulled both hands in toward himself. But his hands never change positions except for moving them toward himself."

"Was this something you've seen Cole's hands do before?"

"No, never."

"Claire, can you use your own hands to show me what it looks like?"

Claire took her hands from beneath the throw. She made a fist with her thumb sticking up. Then she placed her other hand palm up below the fist and pulled both hands to her chest. Beth was glad that she was using both audio and video to record the hand positions.

Quickly, Connor moved over to where Beth was sitting and pointed to her tablet and pen. Beth handed them to him. Connor scribbled, "Is this sign language?"

"Claire, knowing that Cole grew up most of his life unable to speak, do you think this could be sign language? Maybe he's trying to tell you something that he doesn't want the two men to know?"

"I guess he could be, but I have no idea." Claire sounded confused as to what it meant.

"Claire, you told Detective Maxwell that you thought the men were talking in another language. Can you recall and try to pronounce what they're saying to Cole or each other?" Beth asked.

"The man to Cole's left tugged on Cole's elbow and said what sounded to me like 'Ba So!' I think he was talking to the other man in the suit."

"Do you know how to spell the words?"

"No, it sounded to me like 'Ba So.' That's all I remember. They looked like they were from Japan, China, or maybe Korea but I'm not sure which. I'm sorry."

"Claire, you're doing well but I'm going to count to ten. When I get to ten, I want you to be awake and alert."

CHAPTER 35

Connor, Kate, and Sundae went to the district attorney's office with Claire's recorded session. They thought it would convince the DA's office that Cole didn't leave of his own free will. The ADA, Mary Beth Keating, watched the disk on her notebook computer without comment until the session ended.

"This is all very interesting but I'm not sure the DA will go along with this. How do we know that Cole didn't hire someone to make it look like he was abducted to get out of the area?" asked the ADA. "May I keep the disk?"

"ADA Keating, we believe that hand signal means something. We're just not sure what yet. We have someone in the department looking into signing to determine the possible meaning that Cole was trying to give to the young lady at school."

"Look, Connor and Kate. Off the record, I think Cole was set up, too. I think Logan is a jealous man who never grew up. When I talked to his father's attorney, after the beating the man took, that was confirmed. Nonetheless, this is all off the record. Cole was there the night of the fire. The firearm that killed Joel Sawyer and Fletcher Potts was never found, so we have nothing that might link the shooter to the gun. All I can do is talk to the DA, but from what I've heard from the bondsman, his office is moving forward to take possession of Maggie Ortega's house. I'll call you with the DA's decision. Let me know what you find out about whether the hand thing means anything."

The ADA ejected the disk, then closed the lid on her notebook and leaned back in her chair. "Have there been any leads on Cole's whereabouts at all?"

"Nothing."

---

Kate waited at Dan's Coffee and Pastry for her meeting with Brooke Ingram, a sign language interpreter whom Kate had found through the Interpreter Referral Service. Kate had made several calls before reaching Brooke, who agreed to meet with her and review the disk. Kate had the disk on her laptop and queued up to the frame where Cole made the hand gesture that might have been sign language.

Right at ten, a woman in her thirties, wearing a black business suit, walked in. She stopped and looked around. Dan approached her and directed her to Kate.

"Hi, I'm Brooke," the woman said as she approached.

Kate stood, smiled, and shook Brooke's hand. "Detective Kate Stroup. Please have a seat. Did you give Dan your coffee order?"

"Yes, he asked and said he would bring over our orders," said Brooke as she sat across from Kate. She looked around. "This is a really nice place."

"I love their coffee, and the pastries are out of this world," Kate said.

"No pastries for me. I'm getting married in three months and I'd like to fit into my wedding dress," Brooke said.

"Congratulations."

"Thank you."

Dan came to the table. "Your usual," he said to Kate, placing a chocolate mocha latte in front of her. "And an Americano for your friend. May I bring you anything else?"

"No, thank you, Dan. I think we're good," Kate said, taking a sip of her latte.

Brooke took a business card out of her wallet and slid it across to Kate, who looked it over.

"I have six years of experience. I did one year out of state for the court system in Denver, Colorado."

"Thank you. Let me get one of my cards for you," Kate said. She reached into the laptop case, pulled out a business card, and gave it to Brooke.

"This is really great coffee. I need to remember this place," Brooke said.

Kate nodded her agreement and then opened the laptop. She turned the computer around so that it faced Brooke.

"The play, pause, fast forward, and reverse buttons are all at the bottom," Kate said, sliding the computer across the table. "As I explained, the young lady in this video is doing hypnosis in an attempt to recall anything from that day. The consultant is asking her to describe what she saw. She recalled seeing a gesture that the young man made with both hands."

Brooke focused on the notebook computer, then clicked the play button and watched the video. She stopped and replayed it.

"'Help me' is what the lady is describing. The fist with an upward thumb and the other hand, palm up under the fist while pulling it toward his chest, means 'help me.'"

"Are you sure?" Kate asked.

"There can be variations with the left or right hand but the meaning is the same," Brooke said.

Kate pulled out her cellphone and texted Connor: "The hand gesture means 'help me.' Call ADA Keating." Kate took a photo of Brooke's business card and sent that to Connor as well.

"So, as I told you on the phone, we may need you to talk to the DA's office and possibly in court. Is that still okay with you?"

"Of course. May I ask a question? Is the person this lady was describing deaf and mute?"

"No. The man was able to speak and hear when he was young. He can still hear just fine but he lost his ability to talk at a very young age. He has been using writing to communicate. This young lady found an app for his phone that he can use for text to speech. However, his phone and backpack were separated from him that day. Also, we weren't aware that he knew sign language. That came out when we did the hypnosis session," Kate said.

"Is this the guy the news has been showing a photo of?" Brooke asked.

---

Connor and Bob were talking to Logan in the box when the text came in from Kate. Connor looked at his phone and excused himself. In the hallway, he hit the speed dial for ADA Keating, who picked up on the second ring.

"Mary Beth, we just had a professional look at that video. Cole was using sign language, like we thought. It means 'help me.' I'll text you her card. Her name is Brooke Ingram. I just wanted you to have this information. I have to go."

Connor disconnected the call and went back into the box.

"Okay, Logan, why don't we cut all this crap? Just tell us who the two goons were who took Cole. Cole used sign language to message a friend as they were taking him away," Connor said. He handed Bob his smartphone with the text from Kate.

Logan said nothing, so Bob took him back to his cell just as Connor received a group text from Beth asking for a meeting as soon as possible. "I think I may have something for you all. Let me know when we can meet."

CHAPTER 36

Connor, Kate, Bob, Grant, and Sundae were gathered in the conference room just off the detectives' office area. Connor brought in bottled water for everyone along with a water bowl for Sundae. A whiteboard was rolled in with names of the two victims who'd been shot and photos of the house before and after the fire. Cole's photo, as well as Logan's, were taped on the whiteboard along with an aerial photo of the compound labeled the Brotherhood. Beth Ellis came into the room and closed the door behind her. Connor thought Beth looked stressed. He hadn't seen that look since the two of them had worked together when she was an FBI profiler. Beth set her briefcase next to the only empty chair, then walked over to Sundae, who was curled up at Connor's feet. She gave Sundae a pet, then took her seat before removing some paperwork from her briefcase and placing it in front of her.

"This better be good. I had a hair and nail appointment that I had to cancel for this," Bob joked. Everyone laughed.

Beth looked at the whiteboard and gave a heavy, uneasy sigh.

"I'm afraid you need to start from scratch. The only thing that may be correct on your whiteboard is the two victim's names up there." Beth pointed at the whiteboard.

Connor furrowed his brows. "What?" he said, looking at Beth.

"After I did the session with Claire, I got to thinking about what she said. Something just didn't seem right." Beth paused. "My gut feeling was that we were all missing something. I wanted another pair of eyes looking at this.

"I called one of my sources at the bureau. He's been keeping an eye on the Brotherhood. I sent a copy of the video to him. The two Asian men simply don't add up to him or me. You may remember, we have someone on the inside getting intel back to us on the Brotherhood."

Beth paused and the room fell silent.

"What about Logan hiring someone through the Brotherhood to take care of Cole, to get him out of the picture?" Kate asked. "Remember, he told that guy in Florida he had some unfinished business. Could Logan have found someone either in the Brotherhood or outside the group?"

"Could Cole have staged this whole thing himself?" added Grant. "After all, he's facing double homicide charges."

"All good thoughts. At this point, we still don't know for sure. I got a call yesterday about two men who have been on the bureau's radar for about three months. They've been watching these two who are in the U.S. on business from Asia."

Beth stood and passed out a photo of two Asian men.

"Both of these men have been tracked on several occasions to the university that Cole attends. We need to have Claire in here to positively ID them. For the last year or so, Cole had been working on an encryption code that went far beyond anything we know to date. The United States government had been in close contact with one of his professors to hire him as soon as he graduated," Beth said.

"I remember his professor telling me that Cole

had a job offer from the United States government when I went out to ask him to compare Cole's handwriting to the supposed confession note," Connor said. "He told me our government wanted to get Cole before his brilliant mind became a tool for another government or something worse."

"So, what exactly are you saying?" Kate asked. "Cole is in the hands of another country? What are we dealing with here? How in the hell did some foreign country find out about a smart kid from Lakewood? There must be thousands of smart kids across the country like Cole."

Beth stood and paced in front of the whiteboard. "Correct, but according to what we've been hearing, no one has come close to the encryption code that Cole has been working on."

"So, are you saying that Logan sold his brother to another country or the highest bidder?" Bob asked.

"That is a good possibility. At this point, we don't know how they found out about Cole and what he was doing," Beth said. "What we do know is that we're hearing chatter that these two Asian men have an asset they're getting ready to move out of the U.S."

"Okay," Connor said. "I may be able to buy all

that crap. Yes, Cole is smart. He must be an asset to our own government. But why were Joel Sawyer and Fletcher Potts killed and the house set on fire? I'm having trouble wrapping my brain around that one."

"It could be as simple as they knew Cole's close connection to Joel," Beth said. "Remember, this was a child who had been in foster home after foster home, according to what you told me. Would Cole have really ever left Joel? He was the only real family Cole had ever known. So, maybe they decided that if they could get Joel out of the way, Cole would go. Or, possibly, they intended to take Cole on the night of the fire. Joel and Fletcher were simply collateral damage when they got in the way, but Cole got scared and ran. We really don't know at this point."

"I don't know. This is simply too 'James Bond' for Lakewood, if you ask me," Grant said.

"It may be too 'James Bond' for you, Grant, but the bureau knows the two men are getting ready to move an asset. They think it very well could be Cole," Beth said.

"So, if the bureau knows all this, do they also know where Cole is?" Grant asked.

"No, I'm afraid not."

"Are we going to be working with the feds on

this or what?" Connor asked as the room went silent.

Beth thought carefully about how to word her response to the group.

In the silence, Kate thought to herself about how a brilliant young man like Cole could be reduced to a single word, "asset," and Joel and Fletcher referred to as collateral damage. Maybe she needed a new career path.

A knock drew everyone's attention to the conference room door. The door opened and Sandy escorted in a tall, handsome man wearing a black suit.

"Agent Rossdale is here," Sandy said, then quietly left and closed the door.

Everyone looked at Agent Rossdale and then back at Beth.

"Sorry I'm late," Agent Rossdale said.

"Agent Jack Rossdale is heading up the FBI task force," Beth said.

CHAPTER 37

Connor ordered a Philly cheesesteak with fries, then asked for some steak on the side to take home to Sundae. Kate ordered the chicken fajitas with extra avocado. After the waitress left the table with their orders, Kate could see that Connor was upset.

"I can't believe this. They're going to take the lead?" Connor asked.

Kate gazed out the window at the parking lot. It had rained and the asphalt looked like black glass shimmering in the moonlight. A slow drizzle fell and raindrops danced in the puddles.

Kate was worried about Cole. "Connor, we can still be part of the search. And who knows? It may not be another country, with an *asset* like they think."

"I wonder how Logan is doing in the box with Agent Rossdale."

"We'll find out. Rossdale wants another meeting with the group tomorrow at ten," Kate said.

"The bureau sure likes meetings," Connor said disapprovingly just as both phones chimed with a text message. The text read, "Picked up one subject at the school. We will be questioning him, Ross."

"At the school? And what's with 'Ross'?" Connor asked.

"Short for Rossdale, I would guess."

"I figured that. Arrogant, pompous..." Connor stopped his rant when a young couple with a child passed by.

"Wonder what the guy was doing back at Cole's school," Kate said.

Connor tapped out a quick text on his phone: "Do you want us there?"

A reply came back from Rossdale. "No, we got this covered."

Connor fired off another message. "They worked in pairs. You got only one? Do you mind me asking what the guy was doing back at the school if they already got their mark?"

Another chime as the answer came back from

Ross. Connor read the text out loud: "He was tailing a female student."

"Claire!" Both Connor and Kate exclaimed.

"Shit!" Connor got up from the table, waving to the waitress. "Look, we can't stay. We have to cancel our order here," he said as he reached into his wallet and handed her thirty dollars.

"Was it something I did?" the waitress asked.

"No," Connor replied.

"We're with the Lakewood Police Department and we have a call." Kate showed the waitress her credentials as she took off to catch up with Connor.

"Do you still have Claire's phone number in your phone?" Connor asked.

Kate dialed Claire's number as Connor started the car. Connor could hear the phone ringing, even with it pressed to Kates's ear.

"Come on, Claire, answer the damn phone!" Kate said.

"I need an address," Connor said.

"She's not answering. I'll have to call dispatch and have them look on the paperwork," Kate said.

"If they can't find it, try Beth. She also has it. Try texting Claire, too," Connor said.

"If they picked up the guy, she may be safe, right?" Kate asked

"They worked as a pair when they got Cole."

Kate started copying an address on a small piece of paper she'd pulled from her purse. Connor looked over. Seeing it, he gunned the car, heading for Claire's house. Several minutes later, they pulled up to a small apartment complex.

"I don't see her car," Connor said.

"Neither do I," Kate said, looking around.

Connor parked the car and they jumped out. They knocked furiously on the door but no one answered. An elderly woman living next door heard them knocking and stepped outside.

"I haven't seen Claire come home from school yet. Usually, she's home by now."

"Thank you," Kate called out as they headed back to the car.

"Let's backtrack to the school. I assume they'd follow her here after the one guy was picked up. Try her phone again. I'll start back toward the school."

Several minutes later, Connor pulled the car into the school's parking lot. The lot lights stood like sentinels, casting a golden glow.

"There." Kate pointed to Claire's car.

Connor pulled alongside it. They got out and looked at the vehicle. All four doors of the Camry were locked.

"I'll walk around the school, go in and let security know I'm out here," Kate said.

Connor walked around the backside of the building and back out again as Kate and the security guard came out.

"Security checked. Her last class was over about an hour ago," Kate said.

"Call her again."

Kate grabbed her phone and dialed. When she did, the three of them heard the faint sound of a ringtone. Connor looked up and closed his eyes as the muscles in his jaw clenched.

"Keep dialing," Connor commanded.

He headed toward the sound of the ringtone while Kate and the security guard followed him beyond the parking lot fence. As he walked, Connor pulled a small metal tactical flashlight from his jacket pocket. He cast the beam in front of him, moving it from left to right. Soon, he saw the purple backpack he'd seen Claire carrying. It was discarded in the field.

"You can stop calling now. Call Beth at home and tell her to call me ASAP," Connor said to Kate.

Connor put on latex gloves and examined the backpack.

"It's hers. Her phone and student ID are in the bag."

Connor stepped away from Kate and the guard to cool down his temper. While he did, he called and requested that the Lakewood Police Department send out the CSI team to check the parking lot and surrounding area for anything else they could find.

---

The four Lakewood detectives on the case, FBI Agent in Charge Jack Rossdale, and Beth Ellis were all back in the conference room. Before the meeting, Connor asked Beth to talk with him in the hallway outside the room.

"Beth, you threw us under the bus when RossSNAIL and his goons got involved," Connor said, trying to contain his temper.

"You mean Rossdale," Beth said, correcting Connor.

"I know the prick's name, Beth, but now we have a missing girl. I texted him, telling him they worked in pairs and asking him if he needed us to come there. He said no, they could handle this. If this is the way the FBI handles things…" Connor's face was red with anger. He turned away from Beth and walked back into the conference room.

CHAPTER 38

Two days after Claire was reported missing, the FBI released the suspect who'd been picked up at Cole's school. Agent Rossdale knew that the man was a person of interest. However, the FBI decided to release him. When the information got to Connor, he called Beth.

"What the *hell* is Rossdale doing? Has he lost his friggin' mind?" Connor yelled into the phone.

"Hello to you, too, Detective Maxwell," Beth said.

"What the hell could he have been thinking? Oh, I know, he wasn't!" Connor yelled.

"Connor, they released him in the hopes that he would lead the FBI back to where they're holding

Cole and Claire. We did the same thing when you and I worked the Coyote case, or did you forget?"

There was a long moment of silence.

"Beth, why didn't he get us involved? That's the way you and I worked before. I understand they're your friends but Claire was abducted right under their noses while they were busy watching the guy they picked up."

---

Connor set a white chocolate mocha latte in a to-go cup on Kates's desk and then walked around to his own. He put his coffee on his desk, then got Sundae's bowl and filled it with a bottle of water from his desk drawer. He pulled out some reports and began working on them. The elevator chimed and Chris, one of the CSI techs from the crime lab, housed in the basement, stepped out.

"Hey there, good lookin'," Chris called out.

"Careful. I can report you to HR for harassment," Kate said to Chris.

"I wasn't talking to you. I was talking to Sundae. Your ears aren't as soft and long as hers are."

Chris bent down and stroked Sundae's ears. Kate laughed.

"I need to talk to you and Connor," Chris said.

"Is here okay?" Connor asked, looking up from his reports.

"Sure. Come over here. I want to show you something," Chris said as he pulled up a chair to Kate's desk.

Connor rolled his chair over to them. "Whatcha got?"

Chris placed a blue iPhone on Kate's desk. "The day Cole was abducted; we were called to the scene. We inventoried everything in Cole's backpack. Not much of interest except this." Chris held up the iPhone. "I looked through his phone. Took all the data I could to analyze. Nothing really jumped out at me."

Chris hesitated for a moment.

"I was looking mainly for any calls or text messages that may have come in before the abduction to lure him to an area of the school."

"And did you find anything?" Connor asked

"Yes and no. As for texts, pretty much all were traced back to Maggie, Kate, or his professors. In short, all people whom we knew about," Chris said.

"I'm waiting for the yes part," Kate said.

"Hmm...I knew you'd ask." Chris chuckled and hesitated a moment. "As I looked through the phone for anything that would help us find him, like photos or social media, I found the Holy Grail!"

"The Holy Grail?" Connor looked at Chris.

"Cole had a tracking device on something. It was listed on his phone in his Find My app. Whether it's with a friend or at Maggie's house, wherever it is, I can't tell you."

"The only friend we're aware of has also been abducted. That was Claire. So, we can eliminate that one. Explain the tracking device," Connor said.

"Okay. Several of these devices are out there and at a great price, under thirty dollars. They're not really designed to track a person but maybe we could use this to find Cole if he has it with him. And that's a big if."

"You remember that his backpack and phone were tossed out in the lot beyond the school's parking lot, right?" Connor said.

"I do. This device wasn't in the backpack. Let me explain a little more about how this technology works."

"Please do. I'm lost," Kate said. "However, I do remember Maggie telling me that Cole was going to be late for school. That would make her late as well, as she drove him to school each day. He couldn't find his wallet, so Cole got out his smartphone and did something. It showed him where to look. He found it between two of her couch cushions. He told her he had something inside his wallet because he used to misplace the wallet at Joel's, too," Kate said.

"There wasn't a wallet in the backpack, so we may have some hope here," Chris said.

"So, are you saying that if Cole has his wallet with him, you may be able to find him with his phone?" Connor asked, a hopeful note in his voice.

"A few things may hamper us."

"And they are?" Kate asked.

"Cole's device uses U1 precision tracking. This allows the user to find things that normally would not have been found in the past. With the technology that this device has onboard, it can use other, nearby phones to bounce signals from it back to this phone."

"Cole has been missing for days. What if the battery goes dead?" Connor asked.

"Good question. This device is said to have a battery life of about one year, using a CR2032 battery that the user can replace. Now, granted, I understand that Cole's abductors will probably not allow him to go out and buy a new battery. As long as the tag device was purchased within the last year, we should be able to track it but that's assuming his wallet is still with him. Plus, I looked and it shows on the phone how much battery it has left."

Chris sat back in his chair, waiting for Connor or Kate.

"So, is there any way Cole could message us from the device? My friend at the gym has a watch that she can do a ton of things with," Kate asked.

"No, he can't text or call us, but we can try to track him with his phone," Chris said, holding up the iPhone.

"Then what are we waiting for?" Connor asked.

"The phone already has."

"Wait…what?" Connor asked in surprise.

"Look," Chris said, showing the map on Cole's phone. "The device and his phone were separated at the school, it shows that. Now, as long as Cole's abductors didn't toss out his wallet somewhere, I can see where the device is and where it has been. I can also tell the device that it was lost but that would give an audible sound, which we don't want to do. But we can see where the device is."

"Let's go. Chris, can you go with us and work the phone and that map?" Connor asked.

"Sure. I'll let Sandy know."

"Kate, call Bob and Grant. Tell them we'll meet someplace close to the area when we have the address from Chris."

"Do you want me to call Beth and Rossdale?"

CHAPTER 39

Chris jumped into the backseat of the unmarked car with Sundae. With Cole's cellphone in hand, he gave directions to Connor and Kate.

Connor made a left turn on Candlewood Road. Six blocks later, Chris instructed him to turn right on Oak Street, then go two blocks and take another right. They were now traveling south on Second Street.

"It shows the device at 904 Second Street," Chris said to Connor.

Connor drove past the address, carefully surveying the surroundings.

"These are all warehouses. Does it give a suite number?" Connor asked, looking over the backseat for a second at Chris, then back at the endless rows of large green metal rollup doors.

Each suite had a door. Connor guessed these were for receiving deliveries. Next to each large door was a set of ten stairs leading up to a regular walk-in door, which he assumed led to a small office. Regardless, finding Cole safely in this sea of green suites was like looking for a needle in a haystack.

"I could use the UI. That will…"

Connor interrupted. "Chris, speak in plain English. I have no clue what UI means," he said as he looked over the parking lot in front of the warehouse.

"UI stands for user interface. It will show us a map with an arrow pointing in the direction we need to go. It also tells us how many feet away we are from the device. It's extremely useful."

"So, let's do that," Connor said as he swung around the unmarked car and made a U-turn on Second.

"I believe that if we do that, it'll make an audible sound on Cole's end. If they're watching him 24/7 by camera or have someone with him, that will alert them," Chris said.

"There's a large vacant lot over there, across

from the warehouses." Connor pointed. "Tell Bob and Grant to meet us there," he said to Kate.

Kate texted Grant, knowing that Bob usually drove. Connor pulled into the lot and popped the hood on the unmarked unit. Anyone who saw them would simply assume they were having car trouble and had pulled off the busy street. When they arrived, Bob saw what Connor had done. He pulled into the lot so that his car was facing Connor's, as if he were about to jump the battery.

All four detectives, Chris, and Sundae got out and stood by Connor's car to discuss how they could find Cole, and hopefully Claire, without tipping off their captors.

"I thought you said it would pinpoint the location," Bob said to Chris.

"It does show me where the device is, but who knew this one address was a warehouse with dozens of suite numbers? However, the next step I could use may alert them with a sound, which I was just explaining to Connor and Kate."

Connor was deep in thought, digging the toe of his boot in the sand.

"Kate, call Sandy and ask her to reverse-lookup any of the businesses at 904 Second Street. Tell her we need it ASAP," Connor said.

Kate called Sandy, who went to work on any business located at the address. Sandy called back several minutes later and Kate put her on speakerphone so everyone could hear.

"Do you know how many businesses are at that address? There are more suites there than in a See's candy box on Valentine's Day," Sandy joked, trying to lighten the mood.

"We know. That's why Connor wanted your help," Kate said.

"I'm sending all the businesses to your phones as we speak. I was also able to contact the landlord, who sent me a blueprint of the warehouse."

As Sandy spoke, a chorus of text chimes could be heard on all their phones, including Chris'. Connor reviewed the names along with a notation from Sandy that, currently, five suites were unrented.

"Sandy, thank you," Connor said.

"Oh, I almost forgot the red asterisks. I marked three suites that were rented out in the last three months," Sandy informed them.

Kate disconnected the call and they all studied the new information Sandy had just sent to them.

"Couldn't we use Sundae once inside?" Bob asked.

"She's just like the device. When I tell her to find Cole, if she knows where he is, she'll give an audible alert by howling," Connor said.

"What if we take off her ID and badge? Isn't it possible they might think she's a stray that came in off the street looking for food and water? I could follow her with a leash," Kate suggested

"Depending on where they have Cole in the warehouse, she may not be able to pick up his scent," Connor said.

"And Cole can't yell for help," Bob said.

"But Claire can," said Kate.

"She, too, could be silenced, with either drugs or duct tape," Connor said. "I guess we'd better call Beth to let Rossdale know. I really wanted to make sure this device wasn't a wild goose chase that led us to some dumpster in an alley. Nonetheless, two wrongs don't make a right. I'd be upset if Rossdale went blazing in there without us, so give them a call." Connor watched the warehouse for any movement.

"Beth, this is Kate. We're at 904 Second Street. There's a line of warehouses for that address subdivided into multiple suites. We have reason to believe Cole and Claire may be…" Kate stopped talking mid-sentence as she saw Connor and Sundae bolting across Second Street toward the warehouse.

Looking beyond them, she saw an Asian man and another man with grayish hair escorting Cole and Claire to a late model blue car. Connor and Sundae weaved in and out of traffic as brakes screeched and horns blared on Second Street. Bob and Grant jumped into their unit and tried to cross the street. Even with their emergency lights on, traffic refused to get out of the way. Beth could hear the chaos in the background.

"Kate, Kate, is everyone okay?" Beth yelled into the phone, trying to be heard over all the background noise.

Kate tossed her phone to Chris, who almost dropped Cole's phone while trying to catch hers.

"Get in! Give Beth the description of the car, then call Sandy. We need Lakewood PD air support," Kate said in one breath as she slammed the hood and started the car.

CHAPTER 40

Two men led Cole and Claire to a blue Toyota Camry that had been backed in. Their hands were in front of them and looked to have been secured with zip ties. Both Cole and Claire appeared to be lethargic or possibly drugged as they stumbled toward the car. The men put them into the backseat, belted them in, and closed their doors. As the scene unfolded before him, Connor registered one Asian male and one white male.

The gray-haired white male turned and looked Connor straight in the eye before opening the passenger-side door to the car. It was Cole's professor, Luca DeAngelo—the one Connor had asked to verify Cole's handwriting.

"Police, stop!" Connor yelled just as the car

doors slammed shut. "Luca, you won't get away with this!"

Connor heard the door locks engage as he reached the driver-side window.

"POLICE, stop!"

The Asian man behind the wheel smiled at Connor and ignored his demand. The ignition engaged as the driver shifted into drive and pulled away. Connor pulled on the door and beat his fist on the driver-side window but it was to no avail. He tried to hang onto the door handle until the car sped up. Connor and Sundae ran after the car, but they were no match for the vehicle and eventually stopped. Bob had just pulled into the parking lot with Kate aside him. Kate honked and threw open the driver's-side door. Quickly, she got out and into the backseat, calling Sundae to get into the back with her. Sundae took a running jump into the backseat just as Connor engaged the lights and siren and pulled away, which caused the door to slam shut. He was attempting to catch up to the Camry. Bob fell in behind them. A chorus of horns honked as the two unmarked cars pulled out across four lanes of traffic.

"Put your seatbelt on, Chris," Kate instructed as she buckled her own.

Chris's face was paling fast and he looked dazed. He was used to dealing with crime after the fact, not while it was unfolding before him.

"Do you still have Beth on the phone?" Kate asked Chris.

"No, here's your phone." Chris turned and handed Cole's phone to Kate instead of hers.

"This is Cole's phone. Watch their location for us if you can, please," Kate instructed.

Chris handed her phone over the seat and began watching the screen of Cole's phone.

"I can't see them," Connor said. "Can you see anything on Cole's phone?"

Chris blinked several times as if to clear his thoughts but the device was at a standstill on the screen. "No. It's probably due to them as well as us moving. See, to send the signal to this phone, the device needs another phone to be close by."

"We must be losing them. If we were close, any of our phones should help with a signal, right?"

"I think so, but I'm not sure with all of us traveling at this high speed," Chris said, still watching the screen of Cole's phone.

"Kate, can you get in touch with Beth or Rossdale?" Connor asked. "Tell her there was one Asian man, about five feet two, while the other man was one of Cole's professors, Luca DeAngelo. I had talked to him to verify Cole's handwriting, remember? Text Sandy with Luca DeAngelo's name and ask her to run it against any database she can." Connor hit the brakes, seeing a sea of taillights ahead of him.

"Connor, Beth is riding with Rossdale," Kate said. "She said they heard chatter that the asset would be moved today. From what they were able to figure out from the code, they have a private jet waiting at an airstrip by the Lakewood airport. They're en route now. I'll let Bob and Grant know." Kate sent a text to Bob's and Grant's phones.

"Looks like a wreck up ahead. Hang on, I'll take the shoulder."

Connor looked in his rearview and noticed that Bob was following him on the side of the road.

"92, PD, is the Lakewood pilot up for our eye in the sky?" Bob radioed to dispatch.

"Negative. He was working on another case when your request came in," the dispatcher radioed back.

Connor was at a crawl now, trying to get through the gridlock. Other motorists had the same idea of taking the shoulder of the road to get around the wreck. Even with lights and sirens, they were stuck until each car made room to move over and allow the two police cars to pass. Connor took the first driveway he saw and angled the unmarked car up one side of the driveway onto the sidewalk. Bob did the same.

"Holy shit!" Chris exclaimed, reaching for the grab handle at the top of the car's roof and hanging on as if his life depended on it.

Kate worried that the wreck was the Camry traveling at a high speed. Until they could get even with the wreck, they'd have no way of knowing. It could also have been caused by the blue Camry, which may have left the scene. Quickly, she sent a text to the dispatcher and asked if she had details about the accident. The dispatcher answered back. According to the officer on scene, a blue Toyota Camry had pulled in front of a truck, which ran into another car that hit still another. The Camry left the scene of the accident. Kate quickly texted back: "The Camry is the car we're looking for. Did anyone get a license plate number?"

The reply came back: "Yes, it was a rental." Kate texted back to send the plate and information to FBI Agent Rossdale and his team.

"The wreck was caused by the blue Camry,"

Kate said. "They left the scene of a three-car accident."

"Ask dispatch to call Cole's school and tell them that Luca DeAngelo is on the run with Cole and Claire. Ask Sandy if she can get the ADA to get a judge to issue a warrant for Luca DeAngelo's house and school office for us," Connor said.

The unmarked car continued to bounce with the passenger-side tires on the sidewalk and the driver's side on the asphalt. Connor heard Chris start to gag. He lowered the passenger-side window just in time for Chris to throw up out it.

CHAPTER 41

Kate looked at the text from Grant. It read, "Did Chris just toss his cookies?" Kate messaged back with one word—"Affirmative"—and a smiley face emoji, followed by another message: "At least it all went out the window." She knew the guys would never let Chris live this down. It was the typical cop shop banter at the PD.

Connor's unmarked car finally reached the accident scene. Three vehicles were mangled together in an unrecognizable heap left in the blue Camry's wake. Once Connor drove past the wreckage, he gunned the engine, heading for the Lakewood Airport.

"We need an ETA on Rossdale's team," Connor said.

Kate quickly messaged Beth. "Beth says they're behind the wreck on Second Street."

"They're behind us? I assumed they took Edith to Second Street. Tell Beth to see if Rossdale will take any driveway onto the sidewalk like we did until they clear the wreck. That will get them there quicker. Ask her if they know which airstrip their jet is waiting for them at."

Connor dodged in and out of the traffic but the blue Camry was nowhere in sight.

"Kate, text Sandy. Ask her to call airport security with the description of the car and see if they can send out someone to prevent the jet from leaving. Also, ask for any update on our Lakewood helicopter pilot."

"Will do," Kate responded. "Airport security will start checking. Sandy advised Lakewood H1 will be en route in about ten minutes."

"Ten minutes?" Connor asked.

Chris had been carefully watching Cole's phone. Suddenly, he spoke. "They're at the airport now. They're moving…Wait. Now they're at a standstill again. I have a signal showing me that the device is in one place."

Chris kept his eyes on the phone. Connor went through the gate by the airport, then veered off the main street leading into the airport for the departing and arrival flights. Bob and Grant were close behind. From past experience, Connor knew that he had to take this lane to the private hangars.

"Put Sundae's vest on her," Connor told Kate. "Put on yours, too. Chris, take mine but stay in the car until we tell you otherwise. Do you understand?"

"Yes, sir," Chris said.

Kate put her vest on, then put Sundae's vest on her. She handed Connor's vest over the seat to Chris.

"Tell Bob and Grant to get their vests on," Connor said.

Kate sent a text. She was worried, as that left Connor without his bulletproof vest.

"They're moving again. Go to the right."

Chris pointed and Connor drove toward the right around the first two hangars.

"Keep going. It looks like they went past the next hangar," Chris directed.

As they traveled around the next hangar, they saw an airport security car with the driver's side door open and lights flashing. Connor approached the car. As he drove around it, he saw a uniformed man lying face down in front of the vehicle.

"15, PD, be advised, we have an airport security

officer down. By hangar three behind the main airport. 92, did you copy? We need an ambulance at this location," Connor said.

"10-4, 15," Bob said.

"Check the officer. We'll keep going," Connor radioed back.

"They stopped." Chris looked at the phone in his hand, then looked up. Connor stopped the car at an angle about 25 yards from the small jet, using the unmarked car as a shield for protection.

"Everyone, exit out the passenger side of the car. Chris, I want you to squat down next to the back wheel." Chris ran to the rear wheel and squatted down, pulling his legs up to his chest. In the distance, Connor could hear sirens. He could only assume that Sandy had dispatched more units and an ambulance and that Rossdale and his men were on their way. Bob and Grant's unmarked car rolled to a stop at the same angle as Connor's. Connor popped the truck and got out a bullhorn.

"Sandy advises that Lakewood SWAT team two is about five minutes out," Kate said, sitting behind the front wheel with her gun drawn.

"Luca DeAngelo," Connor called out. "All we want is Cole and Claire and you and your friend…"

Connor stopped and ducked as a volley of gunfire rattled his unmarked car.

"Chris, go back to Bob's unit. Sit behind the rear wheel. Just stay down."

Chris crawled back to Bob's car. Bob came forward to Connor.

"Where the hell is Rossdale and the FBI team and SWAT?" Connor asked

Kate sent a message to Sandy. Connor heard the engines on the jet roar to life. The Asian man and Luca DeAngelo used Cole and Claire as human shields to board the Leer jet. Connor shook his head.

"You got be kidding me. Bob, you take out the right rear tires on the jet. I'll take out the front tire. Kate, you take the other rear tires." He paused, then yelled, "NOW!"

Shots rang out. The Learjet went down on tire rims as each tire was shot out. Chris dropped the phone into his lap, made the sign of the cross, plugged his ears, and closed his eyes. The Lear sat helpless on its wheels as it came to a stop.

"I'm sure this isn't in my job description. I'm sure of it," Chris said, shaking his head.

The Lakewood SWAT team rolled up in front of

Connor's car. Men and women in SWAT gear disembarked from the side and ran toward Connor.

"We have two hostages inside the jet, a male and female," Connor said.

"Sandy already sent us their photos. Nice work shooting out the tires," the captain said.

Connor heard another car approaching from behind. He could see that it was Rossdale followed by several FBI SUVs.

"Do we know how many people we have onboard besides the male and female?" Captain Jeters asked.

"The pilot, two men. One is the kid's professor, Luca DeAngelo. Beyond that, it's anyone's guess. The FBI had been watching two Asian men but only one was in the Camry with the professor," Connor replied.

CHAPTER 42

"I had all of the airport runways shut down and halted all air traffic coming in or out of Lakewood," Rossdale told Captain Jeters, the head of the SWAT team.

Another agent walked up to the men. "Do you want the airport evacuated?" he asked Rossdale.

"Not at this time," Rossdale answered and dismissed the agent.

"Were your men watching the other Asian man you released? Captain Jeters and I were trying to figure out how many we may have on the jet," Connor asked Rossdale.

"Here's the thing. We learned the men's names from the intel we were able to pull. They're Chao Lin and Qi Xiang. We followed Lin to a hotel downtown after he was released. We had men posted there. When Kate called Beth, I had our men have the hotel manager open his room and…"

Connor interrupted. "Let me guess. He somehow slipped his leash."

The tone of Connor's voice said that he was upset with the team's work, or lack thereof.

"So, if I understand it, we may have one more Asian man on the jet. We don't know for sure," Captain Jeters said.

Connor looked out over the roof of his car at the jet, thinking. "Is there any way this bird can take off with all the tires blown?" he asked.

"I had my office call the manufacturer. They said they wouldn't be able to get enough ground speed up for take-off," Rossdale answered.

They could hear muffled shouting coming from the jet.

Beth walked over to the group. "I just got word back," she said. "The jet was a chartered flight from Los Angeles. They were told that they were picking up four men and one female. I had the bureau run anything they could on the pilot and the charter company. It appears the pilot is clean, with no ties to the Asians except for this job. The charter company has been in business for over ten years. It caters to the very rich, to jet them off here or there."

"Flight plan filed?" Connor asked.

"They filed one from Los Angeles to Lakewood. From here, they would—or I should say *should*—be filing another before departure," Beth answered.

"Probably one job that pilot wished he would have turned down," Captain Jeters said.

They could hear more muffled shouting coming from the jet. Then the engines turned over.

"Surely they aren't going to try to get that thing off the ground," Connor said, watching with the others as the disabled jet limped, rolled, and thumped a few feet.

The rubber from the blown-out tires prevented the wheels from turning properly.

"I want one armored vehicle parked in front of the jet. The other toward the back. Agent Rossdale, can we get one of your SUVs on each side?" Captain Jeters asked.

Rossdale said nothing, but turned and ordered the two SUVs to the sides of the jet as the large armored SWAT trucks lumbered into place and boxed in the aircraft. Jeters surveyed the scene before him.

"Agent, do you have a hostage negotiator here?"

"We can bring one in," Rossdale replied.

"We don't have time for that. I have one on my team." The captain looked around, then yelled, "Sinclair."

"Yes sir, here sir," Sinclair said.

"Have someone run you to the air traffic control tower. Start your magic talk, son. Keep your earpiece on and mic open so we know what's going on," Captain Jeters said.

Rossdale motioned to Sinclair, then drove him to the tower. Captain Jeters handed a vest to Connor. Once Connor had put on the vest, the captain, Connor, and Sundae went with another armored vehicle toward the jet. They could hear that Sinclair was in place and was attempting to reach the Leer jet pilot by radio. Thus far, there had been no response. The captain took out two specialized listening devices from one of the compartments inside the SWAT vehicle.

"We need one of the guys to attach this to the jet. Hopefully, we'll be able to hear what they're saying."

"I'll do it," Connor said. "Any place in particular you want it?"

"Take both. Put one on each side of the jet…as high as you can reach."

Connor took the listening devices and exited the armored vehicle on the opposite side of the jet. Sundae followed him. He glanced around the front of the SWAT vehicle, then turned back and crawled under the vehicle as Sundae followed him. Once under the jet, he moved and stood on one side of the aircraft. He showed Sundae what he was trying to do. He put one device in her mouth and lifted her.

"What the hell is he doing?" Captain Jeters asked as he watched Connor and the beagle.

Connor lifted Sundae higher over his head. With her suspended above him, he got the devices a few extra inches of height. Bob, Grant, Kate, and Beth watched in amazement as Connor and Sundae carefully placed the devices on each side. Connor and Sundae then returned to the armored vehicle the same way.

"You know, you and that beagle should join our SWAT team. She's pretty handy."

"Where's the SWAT robot today? Did you give it the day off?" Connor asked.

"No. SWAT Team One, the robot, and the helicopter are at a hostage situation on the east side of town. At first, we didn't think anything of it. You know, just another day at work for us. But now we have to wonder if they did this to divert our assets to another situation," Jeters said, petting Sundae.

The captain had turned on what looked to Connor like a theater receiver. They could hear the voices inside the jet.

"It sounds like two Asian men, and also a third man. They're listening to what Sinclair is saying."

"So, do they understand English or is the professor translating?" Connor asked.

"They seem to understand perfectly…Okay, they're now talking to Sinclair," the captain said.

"Are they making any demands?" Connor asked.

"They want another jet brought up aside their jet. They want to leave with Cole. If we don't meet their demands in thirty minutes, they told Sinclair they'll kill the girl," Captain Jeters reported

"Can we get another jet?" Connor asked.

"Wait, what?" Jeters asked.

"I used to fly years ago. I've never flown a jet but I should be able to taxi up to the other jet to make the swap. We'll have an officer or agent hiding in the back of the jet. As they're getting in and I get up to leave, we make our move," Connor suggested.

The captain thought about this as he listened to the exchange inside the jet, with Sinclair trying to negotiate with the men.

Meanwhile, Kate had walked over to Chris, who was visibly shaken.

"You okay?" she asked.

"I'm never leaving the lab again. In fact, I may never go out to investigate a crime scene. I've had enough of the crazy train you guys put me on today!" Chris said.

"Chris, I'm sorry you were with us on this. Really, I am."

"How do you guys deal with this, putting your lives on the line with speeding cars and guns? I could never do this. I just couldn't." Chris shook his head.

"Kate," Bob called out. "Need a word with you."

Kate walked over to Bob.

"Okay, here's the deal. They've decided to bring another jet to them."

"What? They can't do that," Kate said.

"If we don't, they'll kill Claire in thirty minutes." Bob explained their latest plan: "The FBI will have an agent in the back of the jet. Connor will taxi the jet alongside. When Connor gets up to leave, the agent and Connor will attempt to overtake them."

"So, we'll have three men on board?

"No, just Connor and an agent. We think there are only the two Asians and the professor. The FBI believes the pilot is just that and not involved other than to fly the jet."

Kate thought about the information Bob had just given her.

"And us, what are we to do?" Kate asked.

"Connor said to contain the surroundings. SWAT and the FBI have sharpshooters around the armored vehicles. Grant will take Connor and the FBI agent to meet up with the jet.

CHAPTER 43

Claire was the first one to come to after the drug-induced sleep. She remembered one of the men injecting something into her arm while the other held her down. She glanced around her surroundings; her mind still foggy. Claire kept her head down and glanced sideways at Cole. His rhythmic breathing confirmed that he was still asleep.

"Just let the girl go. She's of no use to us," Professor DeAngelo pleaded.

"That's where you're wrong, my friend. If they don't provide another jet for us, I'll kill her. Then the Americans will understand that we mean business. That's the only reason we need her. She is no good use to us, unlike the boy." Chao Lin spoke in English but with a heavy accent.

Claire looked at the jet door. She tried to focus on the diagram on the door, the arrow showing lock and unlock. She had flown many times and recognized the unmistakable smell of jet fuel. She surmised this must be a small aircraft, nothing like a large commercial jet. Claire wondered if she could open the door, jump out, and run. She heard Qi Xiang's voice from the cockpit. He was standing next to the pilot.

---

"We're finding you another jet," said an English-speaking male over the jet's speaker. "You have to understand that we need time to fuel it up. It will be here in about forty-five minutes."

"We want water and food on the jet," Chao Lin demanded.

Sinclair did not respond right away.

"For how many people? We need to know in order to put enough rations on the jet."

"Six people," came the answer.

Connor and the captain looked at each other. Connor calculated: Claire and Cole were two, Professor DeAngelo made three, a pilot four, and the two Asians—it added up to a count of six people. Lin, Xiang, and DeAngelo were the three they had to be concerned with. The authorities were fairly confident that the pilot was not involved other than to fly the jet.

---

"We will provide enough food and water inside the jet, but release the girl or there's no deal," Sinclair told them.

"The jet and food or we kill the girl. Do you understand?" Qi Xiang asked, not backing down from the original demands.

Sinclair said nothing for a few minutes. The silence was deafening as everyone waited.

"Once we see the other jet pulling up, we'll release her but not until then." Everyone heard the anger in Xiang's voice.

Another jet? Who was the man talking over the speaker? Claire was confused by the events unfolding around her. She did know that her captors were two Asian men and Professor DeAngelo. She was unsure about the pilot. She hadn't seen him at the warehouse but was unsure if he was one of them. The few times she looked at him, the pilot appeared to be very nervous, especially when they yelled at him. They had pulled down the window shades so she couldn't see out or determine where she was. Claire had studied many languages and the two Asians didn't know that she was able to understand some of what was said when they talked to each other in Mandarin.

Claire racked her brain to remember the mystery novels she had often read when she was a young girl. She kept asking herself: What would they do?

Captain Jeters looked at Rossdale. "I want a listening device inside the jet in the cockpit, close to the pilot, and also one in the cabin area," the captain said. "Is there any way to have an agent or one of my men lie on the floor behind one of the seats and not be noticeable?"

"It would need to be a small man or woman."

Kate drove Connor and a young FBI agent, Pete Randel, who would be stationed toward the rear of the jet, to another hangar. Along with them, the FBI had equipped the jet with a listening device in the cockpit and two in the body of the jet, under seats. Pete had an earpiece but Connor could not.

The plan was for Connor to taxi alongside the disabled jet, lower the ramp, get up, and walk out. Connor started the engines and began taxiing toward the jet. Agent Randel checked that the earpiece and listening devices were all working.

Connor carefully placed the jet close, but not too close, to the other jet. He gave the hand signal to Randel that they were in place. The sharpshooters were ready and Randel told Sinclair to let them know.

"The jet is alongside. Disembark and board the other," Sinclair told them. One of the Asians carefully lifted a window shade and glanced out.

"Tell those trucks to move farther away. We want the new pilot to fly this one. Tell him to remain in the cockpit. Is that understood?"

Sinclair didn't answer. Instead, his voice could be heard in the cockpit as he relayed the message to Connor.

"Tell them I'm a jet mechanic and can only move aircraft from one hangar to another," Connor said.

Sinclair relayed the information to them. They waited five long minutes. Kate looked on with Sundae by her side. Bob and Grant were in a position to act if someone tried to make a run for it. Finally, the Leer jet slowly lowered its ramp.

"Showtime," Captain Jeters said into the mic.

Cole was sandwiched between the two Asians. There was no way to get a clear shot without endangering Cole. The trio carefully descended the ramp and walked toward the new jet.

The professor, the pilot, and Claire remained in the first jet.

"They were going to kill you anyway," Claire said to the professor.

"How would you know that?"

"I understand their language. Remember, I understand and speak several languages," Claire said.

Connor stepped out to the top of the ramp. Sundae stood still, watching the group of men. As the Asians moved closer, Connor slowly descended the stairs. When he reached the bottom, he took two steps past the men, turned, grabbed the closest one from behind, and covered his mouth. Sundae bolted from the side of the unmarked car. Chao Lin didn't notice her, although the FBI and Lakewood Police did. Lin let Cole fall as he raised his gun toward Connor and Sundae leaped toward Lin.

CHAPTER 44

For a split second, it seemed that everything was moving in slow motion as Connor held Xiang face down on the runway, cuffed him, and took his gun. Standing, he found he was looking down the barrel of a 9mm Glock.

"Can you get a clear shot?" The sharpshooter heard Jeters in his earpiece

"No."

Sundae saw the gun leveled at Connor. She ran, leaped at Lin's gun hand, and sank her teeth deep into his wrist. Taken by surprise, he twisted as a shot rang out from the rooftop of the SWAT vehicle where the sharpshooter was positioned. FBI agent Pete Randel fired a second shot from the top of the second jet's ramp. Sundae fell to the runway, still clinging to Lin's wrist. Connor quickly checked for a pulse on Lin. There was none. Bob, Grant, and Kate ran to Cole and pulled him over to the SWAT vehicle.

Connor ran to the side of the ramp of the first jet, with Sundae on his left. Agent Randel came to the opposite side of the ramp.

"Luca DeAngelo, it's over. Let the girl and the pilot go."

Once again, they waited while minutes that felt more like hours passed. Finally, the pilot emerged with his hands in the air. Rossdale stepped forward and removed the pilot for questioning.

"Luca, let the girl go." Connor waited, then continued speaking. "Professor, you have no pilot so that jet isn't going anywhere. You no longer have Cole. Your plan is over."

Connor could hear struggling from inside and thought DeAngelo either must have restrained Claire or was holding her at gunpoint.

---

"Professor, I heard them. They said they were going to kill you as soon as they could. They only wanted

Cole for his encryption and his mind. They didn't even want me," Claire said.

"You know nothing!" DeAngelo shouted, holding a gun to her temple.

"Maxwell, I'll trade the girl for Cole," DeAngelo yelled out.

Connor shook his head. 'Not again with this standoff,' he thought.

Slowly, Sundae took one step at a time up the ramp. The FBI agent reached out to stop her but Connor shook his head no, indicating to let her go. Once at the top, Sundae disappeared into the jet. Claire saw Sundae but didn't say anything. She kept the professor busy in conversation and tried to pull loose.

Sundae crawled two seats down and came out behind the professor, then crossed over to the opposite side. She realized she didn't have enough room for a running start to jump at the gun hand. Slowly and carefully, Sundae climbed onto a seat back. She waited, calculating the distance to the hand holding the gun.

Connor and Agent Randel waited in silence until they heard DeAngelo scream out in pain and the gun discharge. They rushed up the steps of the jet. Claire stood over the professor, training the gun on him. Connor took the gun from her trembling hand and radioed for Kate. She came aboard and put her arm around Claire, helping her off the jet. Agent Randel cuffed the professor while reading him his rights. Connor looked around for Sundae. She was lying on her side across one of the double seats. Connor stepped over DeAngelo and crossed to Sundae.

"What's wrong, girl?"

"Was she hit?" Randel asked.

"There's no blood," Connor said as he bent down, stroking her ear.

Sundae's breathing was labored and she wouldn't or couldn't move on her own.

"That damn dog. She bit me," DeAngelo said.

Connor carefully picked up Sundae and carried her from the jet down the ramp. Bob, Grant, and Beth saw Connor carrying Sundae and ran to his side.

"We need to get her to a vet. Can someone drive me?" Connor asked.

Bob ran to his unmarked car and brought the unit to Connor. He opened the passenger-side door and they left.

# EPILOGUE

The police and the FBI questioned Chao Lin but he refused to talk. The Chinese government denied any involvement in the abduction attempt.

DeAngelo, on the other hand, struck a deal for a lesser sentence. He told them that Lin and Xiang had contacted him several months earlier, after it was revealed that Cole had not only been able to break one of the strongest encryptions but had also created a new, stronger encryption. The two Asian men came to the university and the three of them went to dinner. Over the meal, Lin and Xiang explained that they would pay DeAngelo twenty-five thousand dollars to start. Once he convinced Cole to leave the United States, they would pay him an additional seventy-five thousand dollars before they left the country. DeAngelo's bank records revealed that his account of the story was correct.

When Connor asked if they were involved in the fire at 2255 Decker Avenue, DeLuca said he himself was not. He did say, however, that he had asked Cole if he would go to China and work there. Cole refused to leave the only father he had ever known, so the Asians realized that they had to get Joel out of the picture. Fletcher Potts, the professor said, was nothing more than collateral damage. DeAngelo said it was never a secret that Logan disliked Cole. He only wanted his father's money. Logan wasn't involved in the fire or the abduction of Cole or Claire. Because the police were focusing on Logan, the true perpetrators were able to stay under the radar.

Once the DA's office was apprised of what had happened, it dropped all charges against Cole Sawyer in the case of the house fire and the murders of Joel Sawyer and Fletcher Potts. A host of charges —including murder, arson, and abduction, to name a few—were filed against Qi Xiang. Professor Luca DeAngelo was charged with being an accessory to the fire and the abductions of Cole and Claire, along with a handful of other charges.

Connor brought Sundae home to heal. He carried her into the bedroom and gently laid her in her bed. He moved a water bowl close by. Connor and Kate checked on her throughout the day and administered her medications. Nonetheless, both of them could see that Sundae wasn't herself.

Two weeks to the day after the shooting at the Lakewood Airport, Connor finished his shift. He drove Kate to her house, then went home. As he unlocked the front door, Sundae came to meet him for the first time. Bending down, he gently pet her. Her side still appeared to be sore where she had two broken ribs and a punctured lung. Somehow, Sundae's vest, which should have protected her, had twisted when she crawled under the seats. When she'd jumped and bitten DeAngelo, he had tried to fling her from his wrist and she had hit the hard metal and plastic armrest of the seat.

The vet told Connor that Sundae needed total rest for the next three weeks. At that time, the vet would reevaluate her condition. However, she didn't think Sundae would be returning to active duty. Connor told the vet that would depend on what Sundae wanted and could handle.

Connor went for a hike in the mountains. He needed time to clear his thoughts. In many ways, he felt like he had failed Cole and Claire. If he had only looked beyond Logan, maybe he would have thought more about the professor and his statement about the government wanting to hire Cole. Connor had always hated to see law enforcement personnel who grabbed from the low-hanging fruit, as he called it. When they looked only at people who lived in the same house or who were related to the victims, they became tunnel-sighted. While Connor was focusing so much attention on Logan, the professor had been right under his nose. Maybe Connor could have put together the pieces of the puzzle. Was he becoming one of those officers who looked only at low-hanging fruit? Sundae was hurt, Cole and Claire could have been killed. He'd missed the clues. He sat high atop a large rock and instinctively reached over to pet Sundae but she wasn't there.

That night, after dinner, he was saddened as he watched Sundae slowly walk from the kitchen to the living room and crawl into her bed. He found himself pleading with God to let Sundae heal and run and play again, even if she couldn't work for the Lakewood Police Department. He wondered: Would she be happy being part of his family as a pet? Without another thought, he walked over to his desk, opened the laptop, and typed a letter of resignation to the Lakewood Police Department. He signed it, sealed it in an envelope, and put it on his desk. He'd present it tomorrow, he told himself as the phone rang.

"Connor, I heard about Sundae," the caller said.

Connor took a few seconds to place the voice. It was Karen Terry, Sundae's trainer.

"Now, don't say another word. I want you and Kate to come over here. I've already talked to Kate and she's waiting for you."

---

Connor picked up Kate, then drove out to the training facility. He wondered what the urgency was. When they arrived, Karen was working with a female beagle. The beagle was still a young pup, playful and full of mischief as Karen tried to teach her commands.

"This little beagle came into the program a few days after I heard about Sundae. I thought of you."

Connor looked at the young beagle as she went through some training commands. Even at this age, she was taller and longer than Sundae by at least an inch and full of energy.

"Her name is Fae. What do you think?"

### -THE END-

A MESSAGE FROM TIM

**I hope you enjoyed this book; if so, please help the author!**

Book reviews are crucial. If you enjoyed reading *Ashes to Ashes* by Timothy Glass, here are a few things that are vital to the success of any author. To help me, tell others about my books. Word-of-mouth "advertising" is the most powerful marketing tool there is. Statistics show it is better than expensive TV commercials or full-page magazine ads. Also, leaving an honest review is the best way to ensure I will be able to keep writing full time. I'd greatly appreciate it if you'd consider leaving a rating for the book and writing a brief review. It doesn't have to be long, a sentence or two will help and is all that is needed.

>I would greatly appreciate it.
>Timothy Glass

ABOUT THE AUTHOR

Timothy Glass was born in Pennsylvania
but grew up in Central New Mexico.
Tim was a first responder for almost nine years to earn money to pay for college.

Tim graduated from the University of New Mexico. He later spent some time in New England and central Florida. Glass is an award-winning author, illustrator, cartoonist, and writing instructor. Tim has worked as a
ghostwriter and a story consultant. Glass started his writing career as a journalist under the pen name of C. Stewart. He has written and published more than 400 nonfiction articles nationally and
internationally for the health and fitness industry. Glass worked as a regular contributing writer for

several New York based magazines. Until the magazine's retirement in the late 1990's, Tim was a freelance journalist for It's a Wrap magazine, a New Mexico entertainment quarterly.

VISIT US ON THE WEB

**Visit Tim's website** at www.timglass.com. Also, don't forget to check out his beagle cartoons at http://www.timglass.com/ Cartoons/

**Join Tim on his fan pages:**

**Facebook:** https://www.facebook.com/pages/Timothy-Glass/146746625258?ref=ts

**Twitter:** www.twitter.com/timothyglass/

**LinkedIn:** http://www.linkedin.com/in/ timothyglass

**Instagram:** https://www.instagram.com/timothy.glass

**Pinterest:** https://www.pinterest.at/timothyglass0417

**Check out our Sleepytown Beagles fabric and wrapping paper:**

VISIT US ON THE WEB

https://www.spoonflower.com/profiles/ sleepy-town_beagles

CPSIA information can be obtained
at www.ICGtesting.com
Printed in the USA
BVHW071454140921
616731BV00001B/16